Pasts Undone

Braided Dimensions Series
~ Book 4 ~

A Novel

Marie Judson

PASTS UNDONE
Text copyright © 2024 by Marie Judson
All rights reserved.

Contact the author for information: www.mariejudson.com

Published in the United States
by Indies United Publishing House, LLC
ISBN: ebook 979-8-9870480-2-3

Listing category for shelving:
Epic Fantasy, Alternate History

Printed in the United States of America

Front cover art by Tatiana Villa

Formatted by The Book Khaleesi
www.thebookkhaleesi.com

Heron bird on Celtic ornament vector courtesy of VectorStock

INDIES UNITED PUBLISHING HOUSE, LLC
P.O. BOX 3071
QUINCY, IL 62305-3071

Books by Marie Judson

Braided Dimensions Series

Braided Dimensions: Book 1
Stretched Across Time: Book 2
Strange Alliances: Book 3
Pasts Undone: Book 4

Lost Xentu Series

Elf Stone of the Neyna: Book 1
A Far Cry: Book 2

Coming Soon!
Missing Moon, Book 3

Reviews for Braided Dimensions

"Fascinating, with well-written characters in a unique, complex world. I absolutely loved this book and look forward to reading more of this series. Fantastic, a must-read!"

—Laure Eccleston

"I thoroughly enjoyed being caught up in this imaginative tale. The characters are compelling. I will be looking forward to the next installment!"

—Bernadette Wulf

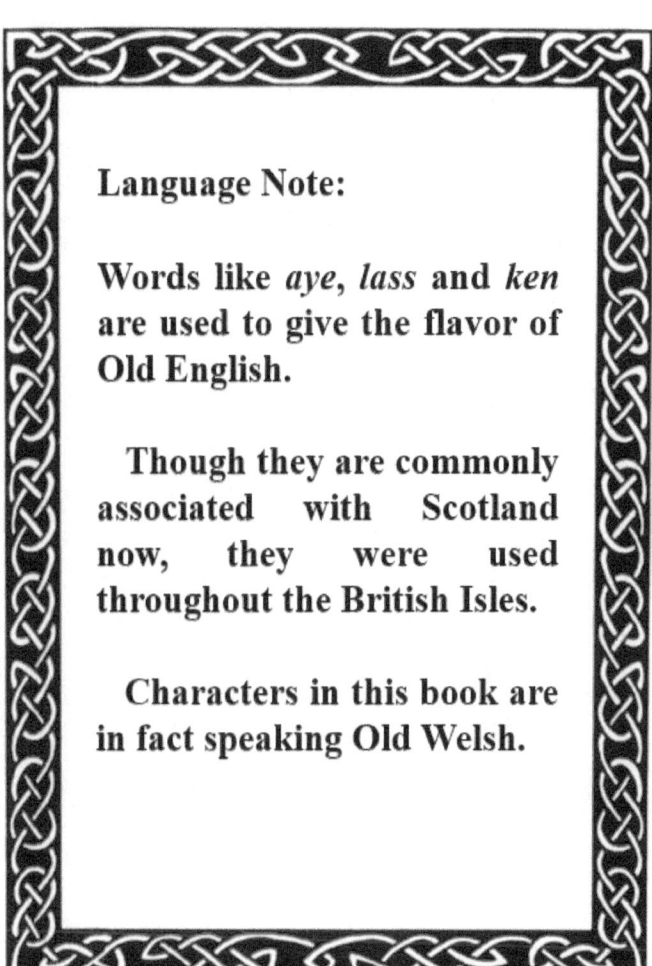

Language Note:

Words like *aye*, *lass* and *ken* are used to give the flavor of Old English.

Though they are commonly associated with Scotland now, they were used throughout the British Isles.

Characters in this book are in fact speaking Old Welsh.

For Piper and Soren

Chapter 1

Rousseau and I watched helpless as Galfride, wizard from the tenth century, grabbed for Marget's son, Ian. We had left Marget's attic moments before and now stood out on the sidewalk, unsure if we should run back up to help. Could we help? Marget, being a medieval Cornish witch of some repute, could probably handle him herself.

My biggest fear, that Galfride would find our time—the twenty-first century—had happened. Now, with Ian's memories restored only the day before, Galfride wanted his boyhood friend back.

I let crucial seconds tick by, gripping my son's arm. "Do you want to go back up there?" he asked.

It had been a rocky road since I first discovered the portal from the tenth century in the old oak tree in Marget's yard. We'd only recently learned that surly Ian of the Celtic band, Harper in the Glen, was Marget's son and that his memory had been erased, his entire upbringing in ancient Cornwall, by his own mother.

We kept watching, staying in Marget's mind but not interrupting. I didn't want to distract her. Suddenly, Galfride vanished out of sight, without any sound or blast of light.

Marget sank to a chair in relief. She could have sent a bolt of lightning through the meddling mage, but in the end, didn't need to. Ylva, our helpful Norwegian shamaness, spoke into my head. "Kay, I pulled Galfride to my home."

I thanked her profusely.

"I want answers, anyway," she responded.

"How long will you keep him?" I asked in thoughts shot back a thousand years to Ylva's medieval time.

"That depends on him."

Rousseau, my grown son, human rights lawyer, was able to hear what I heard by staying in my mind. "Well, that's that, then." He examined my face for corroboration. "Or is it?"

I grimaced. "For now. I'm sure the story isn't ended." I shot Marget a quick mind-message. "Are you okay?'

"Yes," she replied. "I'm sorry it had to end that way after our good work bringing back Ian's memories."

Her son Ian had wandered for a decade—since his teens—in my home town of Pomo Bluffs on the Northern California coast, where we were now, his memories stripped by his own mother in order to keep him from returning to the devilment he and Galfride had been up to, drawing the wrath of the Cornish Council. Lead singer of a local band, he still carried the old Cornish accent of his youth in the nine hundreds.

"I'm sorry, too. I guess it was inevitable. Galfride is obsessed." I could tell her heart was still full from the recent return of her son, despite the near loss again, if Galfride had grabbed him and taken him to the past.

Rousseau and I left Marget's block and walked toward my home. "I guess Galfride and Ian need to try on their friendship, though, at some point. See how it goes."

2

"You think it was wrong to have Ylva interfere?" I pondered, pretty sure it wasn't a mistake. Granted, Ian and Galfride had been close friends in medieval Cornwall, but it was a toxic alliance. In fact, it got Ian and Marget banished from their century, and Ian stripped of his memories to keep him out of Galfride's grip. Galfride had escaped punishment, disappeared into ancient Wales. Meanwhile, Marget had found a portal to my time, through the old oak on Partridge Street.

Rousseau was silent a moment. "Well, no, not after seeing how Galfride can be. He's been fine to me but…"

"I think Marget would like to Ian to be more trained before Galfride is let loose on him," I reasoned.

"And you don't want the three of them teaming up with Thorgisl to obtain the Stone."

"That's for sure."

Thorgisl, powerful Jutland mage, had help me and others captive, in his thirst for the powerful stone, Esch. I'd helped to return the Stone to its mountain home in another dimension, *Sartren*, but was never sure it was safe.

I felt Esch's purring vibration. We'd shared a deep connection, high on *Galdhøpiggen*. The Stone might be wielded to control others, but it had a loving energy like I'd never felt from anything. I constellated my brand, burned into me by Aelfwyn in order to take part in the magical workings of The Thirteen. With it and my other power objects, I'd learned to send a protective sphere around us, hiding our minds from intruders. I wanted to keep any thoughts of the Stone's location hidden.

"It looks awesome, where they are," Rousseau said. "It's hard to believe that realm has such beauty. I thought I saw a city, from the ship. But where Shagfen and Esch are looks like paradise."

We'd not only sent Esch, but also the trader, Shagfen, who'd sold the stone to pirates on commission from Thorgisl, back to their original home, via Ylva's dragons.

"It does. I hope they can stay there safely," I said, secure that Thorgisl wasn't reading our thoughts about the location, though he had seen the ship there in his scrying bowl. Could he put that together and follow them?

"That Shagfen looked pretty hideous, though, with that bloated, stretched face and body. You said our world did that to her?"

"I think so. She already looked better, in the mountain lake."

"But don't you think Thorgisl will retaliate, since you returned the Stone to its home?"

I looped my arm in his. "He seems to be under an enchantment from the baby dragon you saw. It's mother is Amgath and she's watching over both places. I don't know how long Thorgisl will be mesmerized but those creatures can have a great deal of influence. And Amgath reports back to Ylva. She'll keep check on him."

"I don't really trust him with that cute little dragon. He might train it to do…I don't know what. Things."

"Ylva assures me the dragons will keep the upper hand."

"I want to see that little guy again." His face glowed.

It seemed weird, talking of dragons. As a kid, Rousseau had always loved dragons. Now we'd come into contact with them. "I want that, too. I'd like—" I stopped.

"—to visit the Stone?" Rousseau suggested.

"How'd you know?" I laughed, self-conscious of the amount of feeling I still carried from those moments of loving energy with Esch in the ancient mountains of Norway. "But it might have too much influence on me."

He put an arm around me. "It feels loving, though. You haven't noticed anything dark attached to it, have you?"

"No, but what if it felt loving to Otho at first?" I hated to bring doubt but we had to be cautious, after all the malevolence we'd been experiencing. Otho, a brigand of the tenth century, related to Travelers among the Council of The Thirteen, had dragged Rousseau to his time, onto his ship, when he traveled with the Stone, Esch. Pulled to that other realm, Sartren, they'd all nearly suffocated.

"You can get Ylva to scan your mind," he said, and I realized he was just about caught up on what I knew of magic and mind powers.

We stopped at the community gardens to grab a few things from my plot. Solar-powered tiki-lights glowed on plant leaves. Fitful breezes sent eerie shapes into the dark as we passed along fecund paths, the only sounds the leaves rustling and our shoes crunching on wood chips that covered the areas between plots.

Rousseau said, "I'll have to fly to Boston and set things in motion for my move out here. Tie up loose ends."

My heart tightened. "I know. When will you go?" After this, he would not stay with me, would not often join in excursions to Marget's, I was sure. He'd move to the Bay Area; I'd love his closeness after living thousands of miles apart, but this time had been special. He'd learned mind powers, and we'd shared life-changing experiences involved with medieval time.

"I'll come up here regularly," he assured me, maybe sensing my sinking mood.

"Without Boston area's fabulous mass-trans, you'll have to break down and buy a car then," I said.

"Electric, though. I can sometimes take the shuttle, too."

"That's true." *But will you*, I asked myself. I tucked the thought behind the ice wall where I'd learned to hide them.

At my garden plot, by the light of Rousseau's phone, I knelt to pull green onions for our dinner. "Your first car." Though he was in his late twenties, he'd gone to college on the East Coast, then began his career there, and had been content with public transportation.

"Hopefully my last, too. We should be floating in hot air balloons or running our cars like Fred Flintstone."

I laughed, relieved that he hadn't lost his commitment to the Earth.

We collected a few other veggies.

At home, we started dinner but soon Rousseau got on his laptop to make his plane reservation for Sunday.

I added eggplant to stir-fry, then checked in with Marget by mind-speak. "All well there?"

"Yes, we're moving through this," she thought to me. "Ian was angry at first but is beginning to just be happy to have his memories back. He wants to know, since we were able to accomplish it in one afternoon, why I didn't return his memories sooner. I told him Ylva's a very accomplished mind healer. We wanted to do it right, after me bungling the first time and stripping him of all his memories instead of just those of Galfride."

"That's the truth." I wanted to ease my medieval Cornish witch friend's guilt. "Let me know if you want us to come over. Any time."

"Yes. Please do. Your daughter is arriving tomorrow?"

"She is," I responded.

"Then would you all come for lunch or supper tomorrow?"

"Of course. We'd love to. Maybe dinner," I suggested, knowing my daughter, Sophie, wasn't big on early starts and would be driving from the East Bay, a three-hour drive.

As we parted minds, I wondered how Ylva was keeping Galfride captive in her mountain home, a thousand years ago.

Chapter 2

Soph arrived mid-afternoon next day in my Prius, which she was currently borrowing. Rousseau and I had been managing by walking or biking. We filled her in on the process of returning Ian's memories.

"Already? I kind of thought I'd be around for it." Her lip trembled.

I knew her reaction was related to all she was left out of, not being able to travel through time. "It happened very fast, out of our control. Galfride—" I started to say "followed us," but we hadn't even gotten to the part about Rousseau and I traveling to the past together. I hesitated to share that. "—appeared, and demanded to be part of the event. Then Ylva came, to make sure we were safe, and we thought it would be dangerous for Ian to go any longer not knowing everything, and getting training."

"We're going to eat at Marget's tonight," Rousseau added. "Ian'll be there. At least, I assume he will."

We weren't sure if Sophie and Ian were still hanging out together, though her reaction seemed to indicate she still cared.

"Remembering the past," Sophie said, contemplative, "I bet he'll be different."

"It'll be interesting to see," her brother said as we helped bring in her bags from the car.

"We only saw how he was right after," I said, holding the door open.

"How was that?" she asked, shoving herself and her over-full duffle bag through the front doorway. She was never one to under-pack.

"Well, as you'd expect," Rousseau hefted a large, mysterious bag he'd extricated from the trunk, "at first he was mad."

I added, "But you could see the love when he recognized his mom—I mean he really knew her as his mother, after all this time of wiped memories. It was touching." My throat tightened again, remembering.

"It must have been so puzzling for him," Sophie said, brow creased, as we set her belongings in the guest room. "To go from not knowing who he was, to thinking about those years of pain and confusion. And knowing that she did it to him. Even though she felt like it was the only way to protect them."

"Yeah, that sounds awful." Rousseau started toward the door. "Is there more?"

"That's all the big stuff. Oh, I picked up fruits and veggies at the farmer's market. We'd better get those."

We straggled behind her receiving books and a box of mysterious projects to carry in as she pulled out two bags of produce.

"I can't even imagine the sense of betrayal. I've felt like you betrayed us, not telling us you'd been going to the past, Mom, but that's nothing compared to them."

We re-entered the house, following Sophie to the kitchen.

"I guess I kind of had a sense of losing my mom when I came home at Christmas time to see no books on the walls, just weaving stuff." She chuckled as she set bulging cloth bags on the kitchen table and gazed into the living room, toward the loom.

"Guess you're taking over the guest room for the weekend?" Rousseau asked, fingering a plant she'd set on the table.

"I can sleep with Mom," she said. "Isn't that plant cool? It's milkweed."

"Oh, great. You brought Mom a weed." Rousseau snickered.

"Hey, it's the only plant monarch butterflies lay their eggs on. We need more of them."

"Are we in a migration corridor here?" I asked.

"I'll check. Maybe they can divert." She moved the plant pot to the wide windowsill in the breakfast nook. "What time are we going to Marget's? Can I squeeze in a shower?"

"Yes," I said.

Rousseau gave an eye-roll. Sophie's showers were famous for their length and frequency.

It turned out we were six for dinner, not the five expected. When we arrived, Ian seemed normal, maybe less surly, maybe the usual. He was happy to see Sophie and gave her a warm hug. Something was definitely different.

Marget showed us into a dining room I'd never seen before, next to the haunted living room—or so it seemed, being part of the enchantment on the front yard that made it appear either derelict or invisible, depending on the viewer's sight.

We sat around a table with chairs for eight, food already set out, steaming, when a knock came at the front door—a door seldom used, being on the side of the house spelled to appear abandoned.

"Do you want me to get that?" Rousseau asked.

I guessed it was Galfride and surmised he enjoyed breaking form by using the enchanted end of the building—a dilapidated mirage Marget maintained, covered in cobwebs. He entered with Rousseau instantly registering Ian and Sophie seated together. Marget and I sat on the ends. Rousseau offered Galfride the seat next to him.

Marget sent me a thought. "Oh, well. Better, maybe, to have their early times together in our presence."

"I think so," I thought back.

To Rousseau, I sent the mental message, "You know Galfride from more recently. Maybe that will help ease the transition."

My son telegraphed that he understood and would help if he could, as Galfride sat glaring across the table from Ian to Sophie.

Marget introduced Sophie.

She eyed Galfride, her mind full of the stories she'd been told about him. "Hello," she said, a note of hesitation in her voice. "Nice to meet you."

Galfride tilted his head, throwing on his charming smile. "I am delighted to meet *Kay's* daughter." He emphasized my name, flicking a glance at me to highlight, with faint mockery, my past subterfuge. I'd claimed to be Kyna's cousin, of his time. He and Kyna had a steamy past.

"Please," Marget said. "Help yourselves." She lifted a bowl of mashed parsnips which she knew I loved, and passed to Ian on her right.

"Did you bring these from your Cornwall home?" I asked, knowing they weren't in the stores at this season.

She held my gaze and seemed to make a decision. "Yes. I've invited an old friend to live there. She needed a place to stay and I couldn't bear how abandoned it looked."

Ian gazed at his mom, chewing. "I'd like to see it."

His gaze darted to Galfride and they shared a swift smile, though Ian's focus darted away. Galfride's remained on his old friend, waiting to see if Ian would look back at him.

"Does the band play tonight?" I asked Ian.

"Late, yeah." He shoved home baked bread into his mouth with apparent relish.

I suspected it tasted like home to him.

"I'd like to hear yer band," Galfride said.

Ian colored slightly. "It's a good time," he said, aiming for casual, but I detected eagerness to impress his former mate.

"We should all go," Marget said.

"Definitely," Rousseau agreed. "I've never heard them, either. Harper in the Glen?"

"They're great," Sophie said, lifting a second helping of sautéed chard to her plate with silver pinchers. "This is so tasty. Did you grow it?" she asked Marget.

"Your mother brought it from her garden," Marget said. "I have a few vegetables in back but mostly herbs." Her voice was still lilted with the tones of Old Cornwall, even after a decade here in our time. "I'm thinking of taking a plot at the community gardens, just because it looks fun." She winked at me.

"It *is* fun," I said. "We should have a big gathering with Jarl and the rest. Maybe a cookout."

"Like you did last Samhain," Marget said.

"Good idea." Ian turned to Galfride. "How long do you plan to stay?"

Galfride gave him a long look while the rest of us chewed, trying not to feel awkward as the silence lengthened.

I plan to take you back with me.

I caught the thought and wondered if Ian was practiced in hearing mind-speak. Meanwhile, Marget watched Galfride, her heart seeming to sit on the outside of her chest, at the mercy of this man who'd crossed into our time just as she got her son back, and threatened to ruin everything.

Sophie placed her hand on Ian's arm. "I got settled into my place in Berkeley. You have to come see it."

With her touch, Ian jumped as if a spark hit him. He turned and beamed at Sophie, relieved, I thought. "I will. No more stays at my flat?"

Galfride watched closely.

"It's a bit crowded with the rest of the band there, especially the bathroom." She grinned. Catching Galfride's gaze, she turned to me as if for protection. I tried to give her reassurance but she hadn't adopted mind-reading yet.

"So, you got accepted at the uni?" Ian asked.

"Yeah, I already started a summer project." She gave a pleased smile though it wobbled at the edges.

Galfride's intensity was wearing her down, I could tell. She seemed to search for something relevant and safe to say.

"The building is near one of the redwood groves. It's cool. I'll have to take you there, too."

Galfride glanced back and forth between them, his lip threatening to lift in a snarl. I didn't like the way he eyed my daughter, as competitor. I was aware what he could do to those who got in his way, like snatching me to his lair in the French Alps, threatening to steal my memories. Surely he knew he'd be up against formidable foes, though. Not me, but Ylva, Marget, The Thirteen.

"What're ye studyin'?" he asked Sophie.

Maybe it wouldn't be so bad for Ian and Galfride to return to the past and stay? But would I lose Marget as well? I suspected so. She'd come here with Ian to escape the punishments that awaited them with the witches' guild of Cornwall. For Marget, I wanted what seemed like a renewal of interest between Ian and Sophie. For my daughter's safety, I wasn't so sure.

I tasted mashed parsnips and asked Marget what spices she'd added. I didn't hear her answer because suddenly I detected Galfride mind-speaking to Ian about the power stone, trying to pass to him the sense of its potency. He told him about Ylva sending it away to another world, trying to entice him to pursue the stone in the other dimension with him.

Did he let me hear him purposely? Surely he could have guarded the thoughts? Or was my strength in detecting them growing? Ian was frowning, pressing fingers to his temples as if maybe he didn't know what was happening in his mind. Finally, as if frazzled, he blurted, "What feckin' stone?"

Marget stared at her son, then at Galfride while Rousseau and Sophie gazed at Ian with concern. There was pain on his face.

Sophie put her hand on his arm and asked him quietly, "What is it?"

I'd been branded by the Circle of the Thirteen the year before in order to help save the Silwy, Traveler clan with strong ties to the Circle. In the months that followed, I'd taught myself to bring about the power of the brand even when away from the circle's Tower in ancient Wales. I constellated it to create both protection and strength. Marget and I, together, sent healing energy into Ian's mind, letting ripples of gentle vibrations work through him, settling his thoughts and dissipating Galfride's recent mind-speak.

Galfride felt us soothing him and scowled. Abruptly, he stood, his chair scraping back loudly. "I thank ye for the meal." He bowed slightly toward Marget. To Ian, he said, "I'll see you at the Duck 'n Hen tonight." He added a mental message that I couldn't pick up.

Again, Ian's brow furrowed as if with pain. He nodded. "You take care."

Galfride hesitated, then strode out. We heard the front door slam.

Ian's memory of the other man was from years earlier, a younger time in his life. Though familiar, I could tell it was different now. He was mostly a stranger. Ian had experienced a dramatic procedure the day before, bringing back his memories. I couldn't imagine what that would be like but figured it would be disorienting, at the least. He looked drained and pale.

Sophie slipped her hand under his. "Are you okay?"

Rousseau watched, brow furrowed.

"I made dessert," Marget announced. "It used to be one of your favorites, Ian. Cornish cakes with berries and clotted cream. I'll get it." A universal desire to bring a smile and relaxation to one's child through a favored sweet.

We ate the cake, heavy cream poured over, in relative silence except for sounds of delight and compliments.

"We should go inland to one of the rivers tomorrow," Sophie suggested.

Ian and Rousseau perked up.

"The falls." Ian looked at me. "Your mom's been there."

My mind dashed to the time when we made love behind the falls. My cheeks heated with the memory. Reluctantly I also recalled the strange drive home after, with Ian staring at my gold crystal. It had unaccountably chosen that moment to visibly glow under my thin shirt as it beat with the rhythm of my heart. But what did Ian know about the time behind the falls?

"I might have to get Jarl and Joaquin to come along with us. I don't think I could find the place myself," I said, wanting to tear my own thoughts from that occasion of abandon. "It's on a private road."

"That sounds great," Rousseau said, unaware of my discomfort. "My flight's tomorrow night though. I might have to take a rain check. I thought you were driving back down tomorrow, Soph."

"I'm thinking of going Monday, since it's kind of a long drive to just stay one night." She scraped the last of her dessert onto her fork, clearly savoring it.

"You have to find out how to make this, Mom."

"*We* can find out," I said, laughing.

"Yeah, will you share the recipe, Marget? I could make it for my new housemates, too. Make 'em like me." She gave one of her waterfall peals of laughter.

Marget said, "Of course. It would be an honor to impart the makin's o' this family dish. The berries for the real recipe come from Cornwall, though."

"Was this made from medieval Cornish berries?" Sophie asked in a hushed, reverent tone.

"Aye." Marget nodded.

Sophie shook her head. "So amazing. I guess some of

our NorCal berries'll have to do for mine. Hey, Rouss, you should put your flight off a couple of days and meet my roomies."

"I'd love to, but I'll need to catch up with them on my return. My boss is getting impatient. I've done what I could online from here."

"That makes sense. So, you're going to move right away? Have you found a place in the East Bay?" Soph asked.

Ian listened, looking from brother to sister. He glanced at his mom, who'd started collecting plates.

I got up to help and we carried them to the kitchen as the younger folk went on talking, making plans.

We put the dishes to soak together. I kissed Marget's cheek. "We'll see you at the music tonight?"

"See you there," Marget said.

At the back door, Ian bent and kissed Sophie on the forehead, then shook Rousseau's hand. He gave me a quick peck. His focus was on Sophie as we left.

"Does anyone go out the front usually?" Sophie asked as we descended the back stairs into the garden.

"Not really."

"Except Galfride?"

"Except him," I said.

"What a place. It's all so…"

"Mysterious?" Rousseau suggested.

"Magical." She sighed.

At the fence, I said, "I have to bring you out."

When we stood in the park, Sophie was amazed. "Mom, you're like a magician now." She looked a tad leery of the changes in me. She turned to her brother. "Can you do that, too, Rousseau?"

"Haven't learned it by myself," he said, face serious. "But I feel like I'm helping, now." He seemed as reluctant as I to mention all he had learned to do in the past few days, on our eventful trip to medieval time. It was hard to ignore the feeling of all that had happened.

We walked out of the park. Supper had started early and music at the Duck 'n Hen wouldn't start 'til 9p.m. so we sauntered through the neighborhoods and gardens.

At home, while Sophie changed and made herself up, Rousseau and I sat talking in the living room.

"I'm going to miss you being here, sharing life with me," I said.

"I thought everything was resolved but there's still danger, isn't there?" he asked. "I don't guess it has to involve us, if no one pulls me to the past. It all happened a thousand years ago. Whatever outcome it had, it's already had it."

"And yet, I think you're excited by what you've seen. It's hard to turn away from the chance to see another time."

"I can't deny that. But I don't like the danger it puts you in."

"Nor I. I don't like the dangers you've experienced!" I said. "I feel guilty about your being held hostage by Thorgisl."

"I volunteered, remember?"

I checked the protective sphere that encompassed the house, supported by the Sylphs. Then I leaned toward Rousseau, saying quietly, "I've been suspecting that Galfride might team up with Thorgisl. And now, tonight, I heard him sending messages to Ian about the Stone, trying to get him excited about its power. Did you hear that, too?"

"Was that when Ian looked pained and said something about, 'What stone?'" Rousseau asked.

I nodded.

He looked troubled, hearing my suspicions of these new threats. "I don't think Galfride would team with Thorgisl.

He seems to hate him. He wouldn't come when I went to Thorg's tower."

"Have you seen Galfride's fascination with the Jutland mage's rooms?"

"Yeah, for sure. But not when he's in there. Do you think they'd involve Otho? I know Thorgisl has paid Otho to obtain power objects for him but he'd never work with him, I don't think. Not partnered."

Their effort to obtain the Stone had gotten my son pulled to Otho's ragged pirate ship in another dimension of a thousand years ago. Otho seemed to use Rousseau as his chronicler; naturally Otho wanted him on the ship as, in his mind, the wielded the great power stone.

"I'm not sure Otho is the same anymore," I said. "According to Ylva, he's in the South Pacific with his crew, living peacefully on a tropical island. He may even try to return to his Traveler clan, after all this time. Mend bridges."

"Has he been in touch with Boldo?" Rousseau asked, surprised. After all, Otho had been estranged from all his clan, including his cousin Boldo, my friend since the start of my journeying to medieval time with Baird, a bard of many charms who'd kept me searching for the past until I became embroiled in their troubles.

"Yes, Boldo said he has." I stayed in touch with Boldo through the stitching in my boots that he'd made.

"I hope that means he won't pull me to the past again. I'd rather go of my own free will."

I stilled. "I'd rather you didn't go at all."

Rousseau gave me a quick grin, which did nothing to ease my fears but I smiled back.

"But you think Galfride wants to get Ian to join with him and Thorgisl," Rousseau pursued.

"I don't know what they're capable of together. For a while, Galfride seemed interested in helping us, unaccountably. I still don't understand why." I patted his hand. "I'm probably just being paranoid. But I'd like more answers than we have."

"You and me both."

Sophie came out, squeezing her hair dry with a special cloth to protect the curls.

I said, "Guess I'd better get ready," and went to my room to put on a skirt for dancing.

Chapter 3

T he Duck 'n Hen was packed, as was usual for Saturday nights when Harper in the Glen played. Shelley and Joaquin had purloined their favorite table. We entered just as the band finished setting up. Rousseau studied the four members of the musical group, the willowy flautist, Candace of Canada, round-faced harper Sara and red-haired friendly Shane, both of Ireland. And Ian, charismatic though surly lead singer, from Cornwall in the distant past, thin, with long brown-blond hair and slightly crossed front teeth.

"I'll introduce you." Sophie took Rousseau's arm and pulled him toward the raised dais.

I hugged Shelley and Joaquin. We ordered our usual pitcher of dark beer to share, along with salad and pizza. I couldn't help watching for Galfride, glancing around frequently as we danced, sat, talked, and ate. Finally, I spotted him entering the front door. He wouldn't have been missed by anyone, even in his own time, but in this time, he drew every eye in the place. Tall, slender, clad elegantly in fine cloak, finely cut pants and high boots, he cut a dashing figure. As he turned his head slowly, searching, his gaze came to rest on the stage, drawn by the music, perhaps, but more likely by Ian himself.

I studied Galfride from the side, remembering the first time I'd seen his beautiful but terrifying face, in the caves when he drew Kyna from the Winter Faire. As then—as always—his beard was exquisitely trimmed in clean lines, long dark hair fastened back. His olive complexion emphasized hollowed cheeks with just a hint of shadow. His shapely lips curled ever so slightly up at the corners, a bare smile as he took in the band members playing the sounds of old traditional Celtic tunes.

Abruptly, he swung off his cape, examining the walls for a hook. Finding none, he chose a small empty table, flung his folded cape onto a seat, and took the other chair himself. His focus swept back to the band members, and stayed.

I should go over to him, I thought. The more contact I kept, the better for us all. Otherwise, he'd look for an opportunity to be alone with Ian. There was no stopping him, of course. But we needed to stay part of it, this renewal of relationship. I felt certain of that. To keep it healthy was the only power we might have.

Marget entered soon after. I waved to her and she hurried over to us, maneuvering through the crowd.

"He's there," I said, indicating Galfride with a fractional head-tilt.

She nodded, seeing him with her inner sight without looking.

"I was just about to go talk to him," I said.

We turned to the stage, where Ian, Shane, Candace and Sarah played a Scottish ballad with some World Beat added in. Tears welled filled as she watched her son perform.

Sophie leaned forward. "Was he okay after we left?"

Marget posed her own question. "Do you think he seems different?"

"More settled in himself, I think," my perceptive daughter remarked.

Marget nodded. "That's good. Very good." She reached across the table for Sophie's hand. "I'm glad he has your friendship to anchor him."

"He has other friends. The band members." Sophie nodded toward the stage.

"Yes, but you two have a special bond. Something more."

Sophie nodded, skeptical. "I'll do my best."

A young man wearing glasses, sporting dreadlocks and semi-Goth motif, approached the table and asked Soph to dance. She glanced at me, eyebrows raised.

I lifted my chin. "Go on." I smiled, then tested our mind connection. "He's cute. It's just dancing. We'll be out there with you soon."

She stood and moved onto the floor with him.

Shelley got up. "Let's practice our steps," to me. "Marget?"

Jarl and Joaquin joined us. Joaquin had finally relented and learned some of the Old English dances. He liked the jig-like ones best. He taught us Mayan steps on occasion.

At the end of a particularly lively reel, we dropped back into our chairs. I looked around for Sophie, and spotted her at Galfride's table. My heart raced, knowing how he used people. Every worst scenario ran through my mind: most prominently, he tells her he can help her travel to the past. Damn. Her trouble with that had been revealed to him during the memory-retrieving ceremony with Ian.

"Let's bring Shelley to meet Galfride," I suggested to Marget. "It's only polite."

"Good idea."

"The guy in the velvet cape? You know him?" Shelley

had noticed Galfride's entry.

I'd never told any of that crew—Shelley, Jarl, or Joaquin—about the adversary of my first travels to the past. In fact, they knew none of the current struggles. After my original trip with Baird, I'd stopped telling them of subsequent trips. It felt too difficult to explain, too unbelievable. In trying, the numinosity of travel to the past got tainted.

The three of us skirted around active dancers to the ancient mage's table, and stood waiting as he finished a sentence. He glanced sideways, frowning.

"Hey, Mom," Sophie said, "We were talking about the instrument Ian has, the old one."

"T'wouldn't be old in our time," he said, with a meaningful glance to Marget.

"That's right," said Sophie, laughing. She got up. "I told Phil I'd dance with him again." Without guile, oblivious to any tension, she moved toward her waiting partner.

"We thought we'd introduce Shelley. She's one of our close friends, a midwife. She and I grow herbs together," I babbled, trying to fill in enough reasons for our interruption. Interception? Intervention?

Galfride stood part way, bowing a greeting to Shelley. She took a seat by him, having no idea who he was, or that there might be any problem with him. And clearly attracted.

"I remember Kay's drawing of you," she said, a tad breathless.

Galfride pierced me with his deep-set gaze. "A drawing of me. Is this true, Kay? You will show me, won't you?"

My neck prickled with heat. "I don't know when I drew

it, to tell you the truth. I might have made it in the future."

Galfride shrugged. "Yet Shelley has seen it."

Shelley looked back and forth, sensing awkward vibes. She half-stood. "Kay, we wanted to practice our steps. This song would be perfect. Marget?" She held out her hand.

Galfride said, "I know this dance. Will you give me the pleasure?" and offered his hand to Shelley.

Marget and I followed onto the floor where we lined ourselves up. Most dancers were bouncing around with whatever style the music inspired in them. Shelley waved over Jarl and Joaquin. Jarl pulled Rousseau along. We made a good line-up for an Old English dance.

My son loved to dance and was not shy. Even though he had no idea what the steps were, he gamely set about learning, managing with aplomb. Somewhere in the middle, I glanced at Galfride, anticipating a smirk if I drew his attention, but concentrated on Ian.

Ian's were on Sophie. Galfride followed his gaze. There was no smirk.

At the end of the song, Shelley turned as if to go toward Galfride. I pulled her with us to our table instead. "I have to tell you some things about that man."

She raised her brows in question. "He's good-looking. That's for sure. Is he…are you…?"

"Me? No! But he's the one who abducted Kyna's daughter, and his niece. He captured me and was…not nice at all."

Her brows rose higher with each revelation. Past her shoulder, I caught a glimpse of him looking our way. I put up my protective sphere.

"He's not from this time, then," she said.

"He's not. I'd hoped he wouldn't find his way here. I

want him to go back. But he's…he used to know Ian."

She puzzled over this. "Ian isn't from this time either. Is that what you're saying?"

I nodded. "Ian's Marget's son. Marget brought him to this time to get away from…well, partly to break his connection with Galfride. To do that, she had to strip some of his memories. He ended up forgetting about her as well."

"Oh, my god." She absorbed the full weight of this, a mother whose son no longer knows her. "No wonder he was a bit…surly."

"That's right. We've returned his memories. Now Galfride wants to pick up where they left off."

"And…that's bad, I suppose," Shelley guessed.

We stood by the back wall, away from the others.

"As teens, they got up to some harmful mischief— Galfride leading," I explained "He can be bad news. They were threatened with banishment and worse: stripping them of magic. Like healing and…extra-sensory skills." We hadn't really talked about other powers, wicked ones.

She nodded though she looked confused. "I can tell there's a lot more I need to learn about."

By the look on her face, her desire for understanding had more to do with extreme attraction. "I've been wanting to show you the healing and midwifery of that time. I just saw Marget's old home, in Cornwall. And…" I thought hard: had I ever shared with her that I was in Kyna's mind when she was midwifing on my first visits to the past?

"You've just been to Cornwall?"

"In a sense. Though it happened a thousand years ago."

"But not for you," she said. "It just occurred, for you, right?"

I always felt a blend of acceptance and disbelief when I spoke of these things to any of our crew. She was my friend, and now Marget's. I wanted to be honest. And did love sharing it, after such loneliness with it the past years. "So, knowing all that, if you want to invite the viper to our table…" I winked.

"I'll ask Marget what she wants," Shelley said, as we moved back to our group.

At that moment, the musicians took their break. Ian glanced back and forth between our tables on either side of the room, and chose to come with the band to ours.

I wondered what the fall-out would be from that decision. Or would Galfride merely come over too?

Sophie reminded Rousseau of the band members' names.

A new man joined Candace so I imagined there was no issue with jealousy.

Galfride stood. Instead of coming to our table, he aimed for the outer door.

It would be worse to have him angry, I thought. I looked at Rousseau, who was watching Galfride as well.

"Should I invite him to our table?" he asked.

"I'm sure he'd like to get Ian alone," I said. "I mean, of course, you can go talk to him, since you two have been friendly. But…I'm a little worried about his proclivity for abducting people in order to get someone else to come to him."

"You think…?"

"He was sending Ian messages about the Stone at Marget's. I thought you might have caught that, too."

"No. You still have bigger mind powers than me," he said. "I can't always sort others' thoughts from my own."

"That does take a while," I said.

Galfride was almost out the door when he turned and gave Ian a last stare.

"I kind of feel sorry for him," my son said in a low voice meant only for me. "I know that seems ridiculous, but he's been nice to me."

"I know." I worried for Roussseau. He'd been alone with Galfride many times, but he still somewhat doubted his role in nefarious acts, because he hadn't seen them for himself.

On the other hand, Rousseau'd been taught to resist mind control by Ylva—not with Galfride's energy but with equal foes, such as Thorgisl.

Galfride also seemed to have a soft spot for him. I found that almost more disturbing. Maybe I could ask Ylva to search for an answer next time she had access to him. That was another question for Ylva; why had she released him so soon?

Rousseau started to stand, looking at Galfride.

Sophie watched him with alarm. "Mom?" she mouthed.

I gently took Rousseau's arm. "Let him go."

Marget hadn't missed the departure, either.

I said to my kids and Marget, "Let's talk." We moved to the hallway.

"Should we have included Galfride more?"

Sophie asked. "Do you think he'll be angry and want revenge?"

"I know he's been disappointed about Ian," I said. "But we can't control everything."

At that moment, Ian approached us. "Having fun, Mum?" he asked Marget.

She nodded, smiling, and put her hand on his arm. "Wearing myself out. Your band be *rhyfeddol*."

She'd tucked in the Welsh word for "wonderful". We watched to see if he recalled the language. I read the meaning in her mind.

"*Diolch*," he responded without a hitch.

Her grin broadened. "Ye've carried th' sound o' yer time in this music."

There was pride in his voice as he thanked her again. And warmth. But he shifted. "I saw Galfride leave." He smiled at Sophie, but then dropped his voice as he spoke again to his mother. "I don't really know how to connect with him now. I remember our friendship. But it's different. We're men."

I gave Rousseau a thought, "Why don't you and Sophie go home ahead of me. I need to do something with Marget."

He answered in mind-speak, which he was getting good at, "Are you sure?"

"I'll ask Jarl and Joaquin to leave you off. You'll be safe once you're in our house."

"You're worried."

"I know you're friends with Galfride. But when he wants something…"

"I get it."

When I turned back to the group, Marget was saying to Ian, "You were a boy. We hadn't dabbled in mind reading. You're not used to people entering your thoughts. There's much I need to tell you about Galfride since you last knew him. Some of it, Kay knows better than I. If she's willing…might you come to our home soon, Kay, and talk about…what's been happening?"

"Yes. Of course. Now?" The sooner the better, I thought.

"I think we might all be too tired," Marget said, looking at Ian.

Sophie took Ian's arm. "I think you need to hear. There's a lot."

"You know these stories?" he asked. "Then you can tell me."

"I don't know everything. My mom's been the most involved."

"I thought you were galavantin' with some handsome bard named Baird," he said to me, chuckling, his more habitual sardonic personality coming through in the sound and expression.

I recalled the acid-tinged jealousy he'd sometimes displayed. Some might have disappeared now that he had his memories back, but clearly not all. Not yet.

"Let's get together for breakfast tomorrow, and go from there," Marget suggested. She thought, to me only, "We can invite the others if you wish."

"Sounds great," I said, but felt reticent to leave this overnight.

"I have plans tomorrow," Ian said.

"Can you change them 'til later in the day?" Marget asked.

"My first plan was sleeping 'til noon," he said, grinning. "At my own place."

Rousseau said to Sophie, "We're getting a lift home."

Marget and I walked outside with my grown kids. The band stayed. Rousseau and Sophie piled into Joaquin's car and left.

"Are you thinking we should take Ian to Kyna's tower?" Marget asked.

Chapter 4

Yes. I'm going to call to them. I think we need a full council. Gwynedd and Branwyn, too, if possible. We should tell Ian about the help Galfride has provided lately, as well, but he needs to hear all from those who've been affected most by him."

"You're right," Marget said as we went back into the café.

We hung around until the band packed up, wanting to keep an eye on Ian and Galfride's possible return.

Ian came up to us. "Mom, we were going fer a drink. You're not waiting for me, are you?"

"You won't go tonight, son," Marget said, firmly. Then she actually compelled him to walk with us down the block.

At the corner, deserted in all directions, we stepped through time. I had already alerted Baird, Kyna, Ylva, and Aelfwyn that we were bringing Ian, that he had his memories back. I also mentioned I wasn't convinced Galfride couldn't influence him.

It might be too tempting for him to see what power they

could muster together now. Neither did I mention the Stone. We needed a longer conversation about the danger Thorgisl still posed, with or without Galfride.

We stood, the three of us, in Kyna's yard facing the old thatched Welsh home with its small windows and wattle-'n-daub walls.

Ian's brows rose as he recognized the buildings of that earlier time, of his childhood and teens. Kyna and Gwynedd arrived at the front of the house, from two centuries ahead, and walked with us toward the steps.

Aelfwyn, the wizened healer from Baird and Kyna's, with formidable powers, opened the front door and, after greetings, we entered, Baird and his son Hamelyn coming in from the back at the same time. There was much hugging. All greeted Ian. Gwynedd took his hand and kissed his cheek. He appeared awestruck. Branwyn entered the front door holding her infant daughter in her arms. She kissed Ian as well.

I sent thought tendrils into my kids' minds. With relief, I found Sophie already sleeping, and mind-called to Ylva, "Can you bring Rousseau?" He'd be back in his bed in less than twenty minutes. Sophie should never know. At this point, Rousseau needed to hear the full story of Galfride, from the horse's mouth as it were.

In a moment, Ylva and Duff arrived with Rousseau.

"Sophie's asleep," Duff said, confirming my summation.

"Good," I said. "We won't be gone long."

Ian frowned at Ylva. For the first time, he looked like he suspected conspiracy rather than a congenial reunion.

We sat on any chair or surface we could find, including stools from the workshops out back.

Talaith and Boldo arrived; Aelfwyn resorted to magic for a few more seats.

When all were settled, tea in hand, Branwyn began her story; in her adolescence, her uncle Galfride, noticing her mind powers, compelled her mind-control. In the employ of the chieftain at Aberffraw, Galfride used her to help dominate the Isle of Anglesey. He'd suppressed her memories in order to make her malleable. This was the first anyone knew of him after he'd left Cornwall. Ian had been his first experiment in mind control.

I could clearly see the younger man squirming with the memories so recently returned to him.

Gwynedd told how Galfride abducted her by ship— Rousseau mouthed a questioning "Otho?" to me, which I confirmed. She described how he'd held her captive in the caves in the French Alps, unable to move or speak, or call out with her mind.

Rousseau stared at the woman he'd seen as a phantom in the park near Boston last year when she was Galfride's captive, held by a spell in his caverns in the French Alps.

"She was able to reach my son, in our time, though unable to call to anyone of her own century," I said. I told them how her silent screams had come to me in my sleep from a thousand years ago, how I'd found her by spirit-walking in the caves of the French Alps.

Rousseau hadn't known all the details and stared at me. I didn't tell of my own suffering at Galfride's hands. This was enough for now.

"He's caused a lot of pain," Ian said after a pause. At first he'd looked angry, put on the spot, but now the tale had brought him full circle, tying my trips to the past with his own life.

"There's some connection, then, some reason, why Rousseau heard her?" Ian asked.

Aelfyn wanted to get things back on track. "Ye need t'

realize what the man does, and that ye must develop equal skill to detect his mind in yours. We can help ye with this. It cannot be delayed."

Ian looked at me. "He drew you out of the sky, as you were traveling here from your time?"

Well, maybe I had given him some of the story after all.

Kyna said, "He pulled me from the Faire in Machynllydd to his caves in the Gaulish alps." She gave the Welsh town's proper pronunciation—mah-HUNT-leth.

"He paid Otho to kidnap Gwynedd and bring her to him?" he asked. "Why didn't he snatch her the same way he grabbed you?" he asked Kyna.

"Apparently that was started by Ansgor."

"Who drew the attention of Thorgisl," I said, realizing this for the first time.

"That Saxon maggot started a rumor that she'd run off with a merchant." Aelfwyn had been quiet, studying Ian.

Bitter tears welled. "I don't understand why we accepted it at face value." Kyna stared at Baird, whose brows furrowed deeply at the memory.

"Maybe we should bring Galfride here," Ian suggested, "T' explain himself." The Cornish accent I'd always detected and found puzzling was deepening.

"He wanted time to experiment, see what 'er powers were," Kyna said. "And when Otho told him about the magic stitchery…he was even more fascinated." She reached out and patted her daughter's hand.

"The clever lass escaped from the ship by embroidering," Duff, Gwynedd's uncle, proudly explained to Ian, whose brows rose with admiration, glancing from Duff to Gwynedd.

"You've not met everyone, Ian. Duff is my brother," Kyna explained.

"Nice t' meet y'," Ian said, accent thick now. As he took a deep breath, I wondered what tack he'd take from here. His gaze drifted to his mother. "All these years, living without memory in the future, I felt like I was callin' out wi' no one t' call to. Cuz I couldn't recall anyone. Not clearly. When I saw Kay's drawin' o' Galfride, that was one o' the first times I had a sense o' the past. Made me want more. That's why I took it. Made me dead cranky to lose it." He shot *almost* an apology to me.

"The one I don't remember drawing." I could understand, if it was the only thing that brought him a sense of himself, his true self.

"And now..." Aelfwyn wanted to keep on with our task. "Do you wish to gain the powers of your heritage?" I could tell she wanted to say, "Are you with us? Can we trust you? If we train you, where will your heart lie?"

I wanted to ask those questions, too. But if anything, I'd learned that, at some point, we have to trust. Along with being vigilant. Put love and understanding out there, then have faith in what comes of it. And be watchful.

Was he too damaged, too resentful? It sometimes seemed so. We'd need to do healing.

"I want your help, your training," he said, looking around.

Baird nodded to him with encouragement. Others followed with welcoming smiles, though a few frowns crept in.

"Then we will begin." Aelfwyn stood.

I got up and, moving close to her, said, "I don't think you need me here for this. I'll return to my time, if that's alright." I wanted to get back to Sophie. I wouldn't have my kids with me much longer.

"I'll call ye if we need ye." She turned up her cheek for

a kiss. I gave it. Then to Marget, I said, "I'll return home. You'll let me know…?"

"I'll be sendin' you messages."

"Perfect." I felt sudden worry about getting myself home from this time, and looked at Baird.

He came to me. "What is it?"

"Would you come with me and my son to my time?" I asked, sheepish. "I'm still not sure I can do it."

"Yes." He pondered a moment. "Would it be alright if Hamelyn comes as well? Or are ye worried about renewin' that…interest, with yer daughter?"

"I think that'd be lovely."

We took our leave from the rest and, arm in arm, entered the between.

Despite it being night, I aimed us to arrive in my backyard. Baird insisted I be the main one to take us, to gain confidence. I tended to avoid appearing in the front yard, raising suspicions among the neighbors.

We climbed the back steps in the dark. Rousseau took the key from under a flower pot and let us in, though I suspected Baird could make the lock unfasten. He had appeared in my home unbidden before.

"Sophie's sleeping," I said, belatedly, but when I peeked in, she was sitting up with her laptop. "Do you want to grab a robe and come see who's visiting?" I asked.

"Mom. Not Ian? I'm…"

I shook my head.

Startled, she took in first Baird, then Hamelyn, in the living room. She ran to her former lover, dressed in a fuzzy grey wrap, and hugged him.

I felt glad of their reunion, though also worried. My daughter's affair with Hamelyn, in Wales, had lasted some weeks—or was it months—before he sickened from the extended stay in another time. Since then, Sophie had tried to travel to the past of a thousand years ago, but had been unable. Her constitution did not appear to be made for it, though Rousseau and I, after the first few times, traveled between with relative ease.

Rousseau and Baird hugged. They hadn't really had a chance to greet each other in Kyna's home. Rousseau and Hamelyn were officially introduced.

"I think you were with The Thirteen when I was pulled back from the ship," Rousseau said, half questioning.

"I was, yeah, but there was never time…"

"That's when Rousseau was sick, right?" Sophie asked. "And Ylva and Marget helped heal him?"

"That's right," I said. I didn't want to leave her out of what was happening. "Honey, Marget and I took Ian to the past, to learn more about Galfride and the danger he can represent. And to learn mind skills."

"That's a good idea. He did seem pained with Galfride staring at him. I think he was trying to influence him."

"Good observation," I said. "I felt that, too."

"So, you know this Ian," Hamelyn asked Sophie. He hadn't been filled in on that part.

"I'll make us a hot drink," I suggested.

"I'll help," Baird said.

Rousseau, looking back and forth between us, said, "I'll help, too."

Baird and I laughed, leaving Hamelyn and Sophie to catch up.

In the kitchen, Rousseau said, "I'm hungry."

"Of course you are, darling. It's been at least an hour since you last ate," I said.

"I danced. And then travelled to ancient time. Who wouldn't be starved?"

"And walking back and forth to Marget's?"

"The walking's good." He gave me a reassuring smile. "Can I have this leftover burrito?"

"Sure. Baird? Would you like something with your tea?"

He shrugged. "Can't hurt t' have a bit."

The two men settled in the breakfast nook with snacks while I made my "chocolate drink" specialty of cocoa and carob.

Baird sipped it, mulling over the taste as I took some to Hamelyn and my daughter.

"Thanks, Mom." Sophie yawned. "Will you be here in the morning?" she asked Hamelyn.

"I'm afraid not. Ye likely have not the beds anyway," Baird called from the kitchen.

"Can't you guys conjure beds?" Sophie said, almost pouty. "You do every other kind of magic."

"Not every kind," Hamelyn said. "I mostly make instruments."

"Rude, Soph." Rousseau made a face at his sister from the kitchen alcove, through the living room doorway.

"I'm sure we could come up with something," I laughed. I did sometimes wonder the extent of the abilities that floated around in medieval time.

"Hey, but that's a good point," Rousseau said, after swallowing a bite. "Does anyone have, like, conjuring skills? It seems like it's mostly mind stuff, reading thoughts and moving from place to place.

Ylva can grab things from one place to another."

"Gwynedd can create something out of nothing by stitching it," I offered.

Baird said, "We'll come back on the morrow." He finished his drink. "That had a fascinatin' flavor, by the by."

We stood in a group in the living room. Baird took my hand. I thought he was being affectionate, but he said, "This amber ring...I have a similar now." He pressed his to mine. "Do you feel that?"

There was a strong thought-resonance. I nodded.

"When I get back to my time, let's see if we feel the connection." He quirked a smile. "I confess, I've envied you with Boldo and the boots." He wore a bemused expression as the younger people heard his admission.

Sophie said, "What's this about boots?"

"I'll tell you later, sweetie," I said.

Sophie gave me a look, like *I've heard that before*. Then she said, to Baird and Hamelyn, "Rousseau and I are going back to the Bay Area tomorrow. If you stay, Hamelyn, you could see my college. It's a beautiful campus. You've probably never seen a redwood tree."

He spoke quietly. "So ye've moved completely from Aberystwyth?"

"Yes," she said. "I've changed my graduate program to a school here."

"I felt your absence there," he said, face shadowed.

Her gaze dropped to her slippers. Her brow furrowed. She seemed to battle emotions she didn't want to feel. "I didn't realize... I'm back closer to Mom, to where I grew up."

"It were strange, how I c'd feel ye, even across time, when ye first came t' Wales. Even when we were apart, I c'd still sense ye."

Baird, sensing the tension, said, "We c'd stay a bit longer." He took his harp from the bag that always draped at his back and sat, quietly plucking out a tune.

Sophie dropped to the couch, leg crooked so she could turn sideways. Hamelyn sat by her.

"My major is about music and ancient folklore," she said excitedly. "So, I've continued somewhat in the vein of what I started in Aber."

"That's great," Hamelyn responded, turning eagerly to her. I've had more longing lately to return to writing histories, as I did when I was in school in Albion. Da thinks it be wrong t' record things. Makes the stories frozen. But it seems right t' me to preserve them that way, not just in song."

"More cocoa, anyone?" I asked. When everyone shook their heads, I said to Hamelyn, "I remember the blank journal your mom made for you, with tooled leather covering. Remember opening it at the Winter Faire a few years ago?"

"That's right," Hamelyn said. "The year Da last sang there."

I glanced at Baird, questioning. Why would he not have performed since then? He shook his head slightly. Another time.

Hamelyn went on, "I talk with Ma and her doctor friend about starting a place of study, for teaching healing arts and history, and all manner of things. I sometimes wonder if we might be planning the beginnings of the university you attended there," he said to Sophie.

"Mom believes that it was the early beginnings of it." Sophie looked at me. She still nursed the bottom half of her chocolate.

Rousseau and Baird sat across the room.

"I'm sure Da an' I'll return and visit your town with the university another time," Hamelyn promised Soph.

"Your da's been there before," I said, "when I was researching, trying to find what language I'd heard him and Duff speak, trying to get back to your time."

"I was a flea, though. I'd like to see it as a man," Baird said, grinning.

"Sometime I'd like to hear the two of you play," Sophie said. "Rousseau hasn't heard you either."

We all withheld the fact that Rousseau had heard them play with Boldo in Ylva's home. I regretted that I was creating memories with my son that left out Sophie. We avoided hurting her. It caused unease for all of us.

"For now, we must let you sleep." Baird returned his harp to its bag.

"Come on, Da. One song."

"Oh, do you have an instrument here?" Sophie asked.

From a slender bag nearly hidden by the folds of his cape, Hamelyn pulled a small, slender fiddle wrapped in thick padding. He moved to the comfy chair by his father and the two warmed up. Rousseau and I joined Sophie on the couch.

Baird's rich, low voice began a song in Gaelic. Hamelyn joined the melancholy melody for the chorus. Sophie looked enchanted and I wondered if she'd heard him sing like this before.

At the end, they stowed their instruments. We all stood. They promised again to visit soon.

In bed next to my daughter, we talked briefly in the dark about the father and son's visit before her breaths came light and steady.

Then I sent a mind-call to Marget in medieval Wales, asking if all was okay.

She answered that training was going well, but they thought Galfride was close by.

"Of course," I thought. "Are you helping with the training?"

"Yes, they have been kind enough to involve me," she said, humble, though I knew her powers were great.

"Smart enough, more like," I said, wanting to encourage my friend.

When we broke our connection, I called to Ylva and told her of Galfride's mind-messages to Ian, regarding the Stone's powers, and that we'd returned it to its world.

"Was Ian interested?" Ylva asked.

"I think he was overwhelmed. He kind of caught that Galfride was talking about a stone but hasn't been using his mind skills to receive that kind of communication. After that immense overhaul of his memory bank, I'm not sure he's able yet to sort it all out."

"If Galfride knows, Thorgisl might as well. When I'm working with Ian, I'll explain why we returned the Stone, give him a feeling of how happy it is to be back in its natural place. It might be easier if Galfride does come here. We can deal with it all at once."

I heaved a sigh, half relief, half worry.

Soph moved closer to me, her back to me, as if to comfort one of us. Oz jumped onto the bed and settled at our feet.

"That sounds perfect, Ylva. I'll let Marget know."

"I allowed Marget in on the conversation."

"I got it all," Marget said in our minds.

"Okay, well, I'm dead tired. I think I added a few hours on, going back and forth," I said.

"That's true, dear heart. You sleep. We'll tell you all that's happened in the morning."

"Good night…" I trailed off, our connection blending into sleep.

Chapter 5

Morning was gay. I made the kids' their favorite breakfast: crepes stuffed with fresh fruit. Soon they were packing.

"Leave some comfy clothes here for next time," I said to Rousseau. "I've got to figure out more beds for future visits."

"That'd be good."

"No bunk beds," Sophie put in.

We laughed, remembering the graduate apartment when they were young teens and Rousseau seemed to grow a foot in one year.

"I'm thinking a fold-out in the living room," I said.

"Queen sized," Rousseau requested.

"Yes," I agreed.

"What about the attic?" Sophie asked.

"True." I had only thought of it as a room for scrying, like Marget's. What other potentials did the add-on hold?

We were in the back room—what I'd planned early on to be my office, when I first claimed the house my parents left me in Pomo Bluff, a few hours north of San Francisco. When I left the university in disgrace—or what I felt to be humiliation—I'd left my books in boxes and never set up the office. Now it served mostly as a guest room, but slowly a few scholarly volumes were making their way onto the shelves. We heard singing, or more felt it, in our souls.

Sophie ran out the back door and found Bedw hovering in the bushes. She knelt near the sylph, the air spirit who could be seen as a swarm of dots in foliage shadows.

Bedw moved closer, almost overlapping with my daughter. After a while, Sophie stood and came over to us.

"Bedw says there have been attempts to break through our protections."

"Did she say who?"

"Thrizz?" Rousseau asked.

Sophie shook her head. "The big G."

"Right. Galfride. Well, that's helpful. Will she reinforce the sphere around the house?"

"Already has. With others as well, to make it stronger."

I sent Bedw my thanks. She replied with a brilliant trill I felt in my bones.

"Mom, maybe we shouldn't leave. I'm not sure you're safe," Rousseau said.

"I'm going to see if Ylva will visit and explore the situation with me. I'll be fine. You must catch your plane so you can get yourself back here to the West Coast for good." I hugged him.

We carried bags out to the car.

"Not bad leg room," Rousseau said, shoving the passenger seat back as far as it would go, and stretching out his 6'4" frame in the Leaf I'd recently acquired.

Sophie installed herself in the driver's seat for the first stint.

"You two stay safe," I said, choking up.

"How soon is Marget coming back?" Rousseau asked.

"I'm not sure. In fact, I'm wondering if time is the same for her. Maybe because she's from then, it's more equivalent, or she would have been back right after me." I seemed to only be comfortable in the past about five days. Whenever I'd gone to the past for that amount of time, only twenty minutes or less had elapsed in the present. Rousseau experienced the same, as far as I knew. "Anyway, I guess they'll train him as long as he seems to need. They think Galfride is there, outside Kyna's property. He must have searched here first."

"Wow, he's really into Ian, isn't he?" Sophie said.

"I wish I knew what all is on his mind regarding Ian. I'm guessing he pictures having a partner. He has been very alone. I never really thought about it but maybe he's remembering back to his teens when he wasn't on his own. Lately he's been close to anything we've been doing. I haven't figured out if he was searching for belonging, or wants to team up with The Thirteen, for some motive. He always was trying to get Kyna back. Maybe that's still what it is."

"Didn't he used to live in a castle?" Sophie asked. She was enamored with that idea.

"He did," I said.

"Didn't you stay there?" Rousseau asked.

I nodded.

"He doesn't know a lot of other people from that time?" she asked.

"He burned a lot of bridges along the way," I surmised. "And maybe he has trust issues. One's family burning down a village has to leave some baggage."

Both laughed, also cringing.

"Seems like he was doing nefarious deeds for whoever

was in power," Rousseau said as if he knew.

I made a mental note to ask if he had learned something about that. "Anyway, you've got to go. I love you both."

My throat tightened, watching the little car move off down the street and turn right, out of sight.

Returning to the house, I felt the emptiness—freedom, too. What should I do? Weave? I walked to the loom, and sat at it. Constellating my brand, I sent out the safety net, testing from my heart until I reached the very edge of the sylph's protective sphere. I was getting more and more sensitive to the feeling of that boundary, like a membrane. Once certain that, within the space of my home and yard, no one would be able to hear or breach my mind, I began to weave.

Through the morning and into the afternoon, I wove, finally stopping for lunch.

Last time I wove, I'd heard Thorgisl's voice, I ruminated as I prepared myself a salad. Was I able to build a stronger shield the shield stronger by my own ability?

I brought lunch to the backyard and, after a few bites, picked up my phone to call Joaquin.

"Hey there," he answered.

I greeted him and we talked for a bit about the weather and what he'd been up to, which was scattered work. "Well," I said, segueing into my purpose, "if you're looking for a project at the moment, I'd love to show you what I'm thinking of to expand my attic, and maybe create an entrance from the outside." When he was silent, I went on, "like a stairway from the driveway side, and I want to open out the ceiling area, add a raised ceiling toward the backyard, with a small balcony extending from glass doors. Can you do anything like that?" I thought he'd been training to do more than sculpting benches shaped like sea lions, and the beautiful curving shelves he'd made for my yarns.

"I can come look this afternoon," he said.

It worried me that I could not send my protective shield around my kids in the Bay Area. Had Rousseau trained enough to protect himself on his journey to the East Coast? He'd been pulled from back there before, to a very dangerous situation, suffocating on a ship in another world.

I finished my salad and was rinsing dishes when a knock came on the door. Jarl had accompanied Joaquin. I called Shelley, inviting her over to get her opinion on the attic area and we could go over our herb seed orders. With Bedw coming more frequently, I wanted my yard as inviting as possible, with flowering plants that were also medicinal.

We climbed the ladder from the hallway to the attic. Bent over, we crab-walked the length of the attic, collecting cobwebs on shoulders and hair. After a while, Joaquin pronounced there was enough space to build upward. His Mayan friends would do a bang-up job on the reconstruction, he promised.

We walked around the side of the house to think through the outside stairway they'd build. Joaquin and Jarl left with rough plans sketched out. Jarl gave me a quick, last glance as they walked away down the driveway. The early times of near-courtship seemed like a thing of the past now. We hadn't talked about it. We'd never discussed any of it.

Shelley and I wandered to the backyard. "That was fun," she said.

"Planning the attic expansion?"

"Yeah. I love imagining new possibilities."

"I haven't done much of it. My place in Berkeley was already cute as it was. I didn't change anything."

We sat at the round table and diagrammed paths in a notebook, perusing herb catalogues, until she had to go, to get ready for an early work start next day.

I returned to my weaving until Marget called. "Would you join me for dinner?" she asked.

"I'd love to. I think I owe you a meal, though," I responded. "Want to come here? At five-ish?"

She agreed and I started preparing lentil-quinoa pilaf, with a butternut squash side dish.

When Marget arrived, I told her about Bedw's warning that Galfride had tried to breech our protections, that I'd reinforced it more after the sylphs' work in the night, and had not felt Thorgisl's presence when I wove.

"Did it feel different, when you checked it this time?" she asked.

"Yes. I've never felt so sure of the silence within the sphere. Not silence exactly...just pure energy."

"You've gained strength. We still don't know if Thorgisl spied on you before, or you listened to him, but I believe weaving is one of your powers."

"I guess so," I said. "Do you think I block some of the power for my weaving with the stronger protection?"

"Not necessarily. You could pierce through if you were trying." She sounded sure.

"I had another thought. When I go to the past, I'm back within twenty minutes, even if I spend five days there. You were gone almost a day, to the past. How many days was it there?"

"Just less than a day," she said. "So, for me, the time there is still lived minute-for-minute. Fascinating."

I told her about the building plans. "I have to admit I envied Rousseau's admiration of your attic space," I said, chuckling, but I did.

"I inherited the space," she said. "I can take no credit for it."

"You set up the room," I said. "Anyway, I inherited this one. It's much tinier."

When we'd eaten, I offered to walk her home. "I need the exercise."

"If it's what you wish," she said. "We can have a cup of tea and biscuit at my end."

I put on a scarf. It was cloudy out, a wind rising.

"You sure you want to come?"

"Oh, yeah. I like blustery weather," I said.

"Clearly you haven't lived where it freezes."

"Okay. That's fair." I laughed.

We walked briskly, chummy.

"Tell me how things went with Ian."

She described Ylva's efforts to discover what might weaken him with Galfride. It sounded very much like her work with Rousseau and me, helping him to know when the other man was in his head and to repulse influences.

At her home, she made a blaze in the wood-burner and we sat companionably.

"Did Ian return to Berkeley?"

"He did."

"Can you tell if Galfride came back when you returned?"

"I haven't detected him. I'm wondering about you walking home. Perhaps you should just transport yourself this time. You had walk enough on the way."

"It's a thought. I'm not that afraid of Galfride anymore. But it might be false complacency."

"Let's scry," she said.

So, we climbed to the attic room and uncovered the black bowl. I wanted more practice anyway. I constellated my brand—a literal scar burned onto my shoulder, in the shape of an archaic stylized heron. It was in fact quite beautiful, designed by Aelfwyn and Kyna's brother, Duff. I'd learned to use it, along with my rings and silver triadic pendant, to manifest my will. This time I applied it for sight. Touching the water and sending energy from my heart, through the brand, to the rings and into the water. we sent our intent to see where Galfride was.

Instead, Thorgisl appeared on the surface of the scrying bowl.

Chapter 6

He petted a beguiling creature a few feet long, with a twisting tail and crystalline scales shot through with coursing hues. "Ah, good day, ladies. Kay, I think you've met Frigon."

The dragon had grown so much. Again, I wondered about the wisdom of giving him such a pet. But Ylva could never take him back. That would be a source of rage we could not even contemplate, obviously, by the way he looked at it.

"You thought this offering would make me forget the stone." He gave a mirthless laugh.

Feeling unqualified to deal with the Jutlander alone, I gave Ylva a mind-call.

I had thought she might appear on the water but, instead, she stood in Marget's attic room.

We withdrew from the water. I created a protected cone. "Thorgisl came to our scrying when we were trying to find Galfride."

Thorgisl broke through my cone. "You search for Galfride? He's here."

It was what I'd feared. The two who had been enemies were forming an alliance. They sought the Stone. And now their force could break through our defenses.

Ylva struck out a hand and we no longer heard the Jutlander. For the moment. But what would be the price of sending him away without dealing with the issues?

I was shaking. Ylva put an arm around me.

"What does this mean?" I asked. "Do you think Galfride wants Thorgisl's help in drawing Ian? He could promise to make him an apprentice mage and help them obtain the Stone."

"We will work together to see all," Ylva assured me.

Marget wrung her hands; she was a hedge witch extraordinaire, and a savvy coder on the dark web, but dealing with a mage like this was new territory. She had her son back at last. But for how long?

Ylva drew a small vial from one of her immense pockets, knelt by the bowl, and dripped oil on the water. It spread quickly, a light mist rose.

Marget's scrying bowl was not as large as Thorgisl's. The three of us could hold hands as we sat around it. The mist increased until a scene formed and shifted. We saw Thorgisl and Galfride in the tower room at the Jutland fort. The scene shifted and we saw— Oh! Ian and Sophie in bed together at her apartment. We exchanged glances, grins suppressed.

Well, that took care of one question. For the moment.

The vision returned to the Jutland tower. We spied as the two men conjectured on Otho's role in the latest Stone movement. Soon Galfride left.

Ylva let the misty image fall away.

"We need to be proactive. Tell him…" I said.

"Where the stone is? That it's happy now? Do you think he cares?" Ylva asked.

"I think Kay is right that we should act rather than sit and wait," Marget said.

Ylva was quiet a moment. Then she said, "Through the dragon I have access to Thorgisl's doings. I can speak to him through his dragon as well. I will work on this. It is to all our interests that the Stone does not get into Thorgisl's hands."

"Tell us what we need to do," I said, willing to relinquish the actual strategizing.

"It's good that your son is building a love-tie in this world," Ylva said to Marget.

"Yes, it seems positive," Marget said. "I hope you're happy about it," she added, to me.

"I think so." I had to be honest. How could I be over-the-moon about it when Galfride was still trying to influence Ian, and might see my daughter as an obstacle. "Ian might be happy that Sophie can't time-travel. I am, as well, at times, though there's the danger that he could try to force it and harm her. He was so angry when he knew I'd gone to the past, even before he got his memories back. He said to me, 'Why should it be you?'"

The two women seemed to take this in.

"Kay, you have not furthered your tie with your heron, have you?" Marget asked.

Ylva looked amused.

"As a matter of fact, on Ylva's mountainside, I shifted into my spirit animal." The numinous feeling of those moments as we walked together—Ylva as wolf, I as heron—rushed back to me, taking my breath away for a moment.

"Have you arrived at a point where you're able to manifest the shift deliberately?" Marget asked.

Ylva raised her brows with interest.

"No. I wish," I said.

Ylva suggested that she escort me home. We said good-night to Marget and started through the neighborhood. I'd never walked with Ylva along these blocks in my town. I pointed out the gardens as we passed.

"This is where the herbs are grown, that you brought to me?" she asked.

"Yes."

Ylva's night vision was extraordinary, probably from having been many nocturnal animals. She wanted to walk through the gardens, so we did. In Shelley's patch, surrounded by rare and amazing plants, Ylva squatted and touched leaves, tasted some, in the shape of an archaic stylized heron, sniffed others. She broke a leaf and rubbed it, then continued through the small leafy labyrinth, doing the same throughout.

"Your heron would like it here. Have you the small carving I made?"

"Yes, I carry it everywhere." I pulled the smooth, palm-sized stone carving from my cape pocket.

We sat on a carpet of clover grass in one corner and held hands, the carving between us.

"Each time you do this, the amulet's power to call her will increase," Ylva said, quietly.

After a moment, a luminosity formed against the backdrop of foliage. My heron. Tall. Gangling. And beautiful. More iridescent than the first time I'd seen her, in the café. My heart raced.

"Now, feel her energy. What does she say to you?"

I slowed my breathing and listened. When I constellated my brand, she became more distinct. She ducked her head, long sinuous neck bending, like in the brand. She seemed to say, "Yes, I am on your back. And in the air near you. Always."

My guide, if I could let my awareness expand to her. I

noticed Bedw then, fluttering, moving-dots, among the plant leaves near the spirit heron, as my sight adjusted to the dark. Other beings were there as well.

"Call me by Hegri. Know me." I felt the ideas as thoughts. Could I hear a voice?

It was different from forming mind-bonds with humans, more like the language of dreams: images, sensations, the expanded sense-world we experience only in sleep but have a hard time bringing back with us to the waking world. I felt I would never fully understand but could grow closer, more attuned. There was a caring sense, like the one in dreams, so hard to describe yet more real than most earthly connections.

"Yes, that is what we share." Her bird eye imparted the sentience of dream animals; therefore, I felt it on the soul level.

I could have gone on that way long into the night, and hated the thought of breaking the tie but, conscious of Ylva's presence, I brought myself back. After a moment of adjustment, I said, "I hope I can do that myself."

"You can," she responded, as we pushed ourselves to standing.

"What about shifting into her again?"

"That will be Hegri's choice, in part. She is you. You are her. She will see when there is need. That is what I find with my wolf."

"I'm almost afraid I'll want to stay her. It's such a beautiful sensation."

"You can't. But you can have something else."

"What's that?" I asked, as we began walking.

"Some of her that stays in you. A power that grows."

Looking over my shoulder, I saw Hegri stalking behind us and felt relief.

"Do you keep your spirit animals all the time?" I asked.

"Some, yes. They are always there. I forget, and then remember."

"Some that are in other worlds?"

"They are all in other worlds. And in this one," she said.

I felt daunted by her ephemeral knowledge. "I saw the Stone, and its happiness. I want it to stay there, safe," Tears welled up, surprising me.

"I feel the same." Ylva took my hand, hers warm and engulfing.

"Can you tell if that world knows where Shagfen and the Stone are?"

"Amgath checks. She helps Shagfen and the nyad grow healthier."

"She can survive, there in the mountain? She has what she needs to eat and so on?"

"I believe so. Whether she can remain without contact with her kind is another matter. I hope her nyad clan finds her, but none who will betray her. They are not accepted by the religion that is in power there. I imagine, though, that, since her experiences on Earth, for a while at least, she'll be happy to be alone and healthy."

"That makes sense," I said. "But—"

"I know. You worry that Thorgisl is joining with others."

"You know of someone other than Galfride?"

"Galfride has been in contact with Ansgor."

I stopped. That had been my worst dread the first year I knew anything of Baird's time. The three villains— Galfride, Ansgor, and Thorgisl—might all now work together? I pushed away the thought.

"What's happening with Otho?"

"The sea captain is trying to stay far from all of them. I put fear in him of Thorgisl and Galfride. He stays in the tropical place and is happy there."

"Can you help him shield? Does he have that talent?"

"He has always had that skill. He was being greedy before. I've helped to convert the Stone's energy in him to its loving form."

I stared at Ylva as we drew near my home. "That's brilliant."

"Yes, I think he loves the Stone as much as we do. I believe he is changing."

I laughed, happy. And thought then that I heard the heron's call, rejoicing with me. I turned, and in the darkness, saw her light form silhouetted against a tree in my yard. Joy swept through me, and in that moment, felt like for always. I let that rest in me, not allowing doubt.

"I will bid you good-night," Ylva said, and bent down to kiss my cheek. She called then to my hegri. It sounded like a clicking "Tscho, tscho," and then she was gone.

I walked toward my front door. What kind of call could I send to my soul-bird? Would she ever tell me? I waved to her, an inadequate gesture, and let myself into my house.

Chapter 7

My first night without kids in the house, I decided on a bubble bath. When I'd soaked and climbed into bed in a fresh nightgown, Oz jumped up and lay at my feet. I stilled my mind and called to Rousseau. "Have you arrived safely?"

"Yes," he answered immediately. "This is great. No cell phone needed."

"Well, we'll still want to share photos beyond the two of us," I said, smiling. "I have news." I caught him up on what I'd learned, first from Marget, then from Ylva.

"That's great about Otho," he said. "It might mean he won't pull me to the past again."

"True." I wanted him to relax in that knowledge. On the other hand, it would not do for him to be caught unaware. "I think Ylva will need to train you to sense Galfride. Even Ansgor. I suspect the three might be building a power circle of their own,. That's always been the Saxon mage's desire."

"That's what they wanted Kyna for? Not good."

"I don't mean to worry you," I said. "We're trying to reach a point where we no longer have to be wary but—"

"The concerns still exist," he said. "I'm going to pack quickly. I've decided to put my things in storage in the East

Bay and stay with you as long as needed for this to be over."

Warmth bloomed in my heart. "I'd like that. You being separate on the East Coast or in the East Bay worries me. I'd feel better with you close while you're still learning."

"Me, too, Mom."

I told him about the further work we'd done with my totem. "You know how you were drawn to the dragon? I wonder if Ylva could help you find one as a spirit animal. I don't know if they have to choose you or if you can court the relationship."

I felt Rousseau's deep breath. "That sounds amazing."

"Let's explore it. I'm going to sleep. Let me know when you have things together and the date for your return flight. It's worked out with your job, for you to leave?"

"It has, I'm tying up loose ends now, passing my clients to others."

"Do you feel okay about it?" I asked.

He affirmed that he did, said good night.

Next day, I finished weaving and took the cloth from the loom. I had purposely not examined what I was creating, preferring to let it emerge and then see. I spread it on my work table, and recognized Esch's cave. No wonder I had wanted to save it from Thorgisl's vision.

I jumped, realizing I suddenly knew the Stone's name. Had it told me during the weaving?

The scene depicted was a brilliant play of gold-green light, with Amgath the dragon playing in the waters of the luminous, azure pool, surrounded by lush ferns. Multicolored butterflies, bright frogs, and iridescent salamanders moved among the rocks and plants. In a hollow, the Stone glowed amber.

I felt the Stone's love, and wished the weaving might protect the area it depicted. If I had Gwynnedd's talent with stitchery maybe it could. I should ask her to embroider power into it. For some reason, I assumed I'd been compelled to weave the scene for a purpose.

It took me a few moments of gazing to notice the water creature tucked in among flowering vines. Shagfen. Ylva had called her a nyad. Her form was now astoundingly sleek, vivid, with shades of cerulean and jade tinged with warm golden brown. Her appearance here on earth had been grotesque, hugely bloated and miserable. Now the wide features of her face had formed into compelling contours, darkly lined. She was magnificent.

Where to keep the hanging? The way the design had come to me in my weaving, I feared—maybe hoped as well—that it might be a sort of portal to Esch and Shagen. It should be safe, I thought, if I hung it on the living room wall. The sylphs were constantly shoring up the protections on the sphere around the house.

I took up the cloth, carefully reinforced the edges, then wound it over a wood pole, adding a string to hang it. But I needed advice on it. Other than me, Ylva was the most invested in protecting Esch, and would appreciate seeing the tapestry. I spoke to her in my mind.

"Ylva, are you busy?"

She responded sleepily, "*Félagi?*"

Old Norse for mate, partner or fellow traveler. I detected the meaning from her mind, at the same time realizing I'd woken her.

"Give me a moment," she said.

I watched in her mind as she climbed from her bed, where Duff formed a sizable mound that snored. She descended the stairs, bundling herself in a long wool cape as she went, stepping out into dawn-pink light that hit her mountains.

All the while, I protested, "Ylva, you don't need to get up! I can talk with you later."

"There's something you're excited about, *nipt.*" She called me sister. "You've done something for our Stone."

"I have, without knowing," I said. "It gave me its name. I think it did, anyway." I was reluctant to send the name to her, even in our dedicated communication, mind-to-mind.

"Show me," she said.

I stood in front of the new hanging I'd woven. She gasped small excited breaths, mumbling about each part. "Look at the Stone in its grotto. Just like I saw it. Small beautiful animals. Amgath frolicking in the pool. Shagfen. Is that her…in the leaves, shadowed? Get closer."

I stepped within inches, my gaze moving directly to the shadowed creature.

"Put a little globe light over it," she said.

I hadn't made one on my own before. Putting out my hand, I thought about the feeling of holding the illumination. A tiny ball of light suddenly hovered over my palm. I sucked in a startled breath.

"Yes." Ylva grinned as I moved it to the part of the cloth she wanted to see. "She's amazing. I hadn't imagined. I only got a glimpse before."

"Isn't she exquisite? It occurred to me that my weaving might help them stay safe. If it remains a safe scene, might they be kept from harm? Like Gwynedd can make things true. Do you think so, or is it hubris?"

She laughed. "I like that word. Shamans need to avoid hubris. But some helps." She sobered. "There is importance to what you have made. We do not know all its power yet. I must visit the cloth in person to ascertain more, put my hands on it." She thought a moment. "Do you think you might make an identical cloth for me?"

"I can try. Though these cloths sort of weave themselves. I'm not sure if it would come out differently for you."

"Then that would be of interest as well," she said. She was silent a moment. "I wonder if Gwynedd's ability might work for something that takes only a moment. Can it be an ongoing effect? We need to ask her what she's observed."

"Maybe if you come here, you might know how I could build more power into it. Or get someone's help."

"There are others who know quite a lot about the power of weaving. Such as Kyna. Aren't there?"

"I think so. Marget likely knows a lot, too. I saw a loom in her home in Cornwall. I thought Gwynedd might embroider magic into it."

"You must be careful with that. She does not know Esch as you do."

Had I told her the Stone's name?

Ylva seemed to have heard me and answered. "I heard it in your mind right away. It feels right."

Well, that took away the need to decide in what circumstance I could safely tell her the Stone's name. "I have another question."

She sat on a stone slab where I'd sat with her not long before, in her time.

"My son is drawn to the dragon baby you gave Thorgisl. Is it possible for him to court a dragon as a totem or spirit animal? I know he's dedicated to learning but... that could be an extra motivation."

"Your son must come and train with me. If he wants to court a spirit animal, especially a dragon, that will take much work," she said.

"I'm sure he'd like that. Are you willing to take the time?"

"Of course. I want to."

My heart soared. "I'm hoping, in the training, you can help him sense any of the those who might come into his mind with ill purpose, and repulse them? Ansgor, for instance."

"You remind me. I must visit the Saxon. I have business with him. Yes, Kay. I will train Rousseau fully in sensing any new presence in his mind, and protecting himself. When will he come?"

"He's in the midst of moving closer to me. I'm sure very soon."

"You are worried about this attempted alliance between Galfride, Ansgor, and Thrizzle."

"Yes. You're not?"

"I have my watch on Thorgisl's fort, and sense his communications. You and Marget have to set monitors to detect Galfride's movements in your time. Try to predict anywhere he might go. We should ask Aelfwyn to do the same in her area. Do we know if he's detected Kyna's century yet?"

"He seems mostly interested in Ian right now. I imagine he might go wherever Marget and her son go."

"Ah. Ian. He will need more training as well. Should we join him together with Rousseau? Your boy seems solid but might help to convince the other young man."

It would be a very different situation, convincing Ian to shut Galfride out, than getting my son capable of and willing to repulse Otho and Thorgisl. "How much did you do with Ian, with Aelfwyn in Kyna's tower?"

"We examined the ties he might still feel to Galfride and worked with the inner landscape of his mind, to understand just what Galfride had been doing there. Where he might fail in his ethics. Where Ian comes to stand might fall to fate but we can do our best to predict and prevent. Honestly, I did not feel excessive warmth in Ian for Galfride."

"But we know Galfride has immense powers of persuasion and Ian has felt lost for a very long time, forsaken by his mom, his only family," I said.

"It will be imperative to keep trying to convince Ian to be trained. We might frame it positively. 'Think of the powers you had as a child that might be renewed.' We did begin, just the very rudiments: being aware of entrance to his mind, some control to shut away his memories, keep them safe. I think that much felt intuitive for him and he welcomed the review."

"That's good. Really good. It might be all we can do for now. You're right. He will become who he'll become. It's just, there was so much anger when I first knew him. I don't want Galfride to attach to that and use it for his own gain."

"We did find pockets of that. Much was over the sense of alienation, belonging nowhere, missing his mother. And her apparent betrayal. We worked through those. Some of his surliness is just him. I can train the young men separately, though, if you think it advisable."

"Let's start that way and you could decide based on what you find. I'm sorry it would take more time. We're taking too much of your attention from your people."

"Their safety is involved with all this. I do it by choice."

"Thank you, Ylva. I don't know what we would have—"

"I love you, too. I will start my day now, see if Duff is eating yet."

We parted, and I tapped a hello in my son's mind, knowing it was a more seemly hour for him.

"Hey, Mama. What's up?"

"Would you prefer I call or text?"

"No, I love this. It makes me feel close to you. Besides, I like to practice."

"That's good because Ylva said she'll train you."

"Great!"

"She said that all of work would be necessary for you to find a dragon as spirit animal."

"It's possible though?" he asked, a tad breathless.

I grinned. "Seems like it. How's the move going?"

"I've packed what I'm bringing. I'll give away a lot and send the rest. Be out to California in a week."

"Marvelous," I said. "Can I help in some way?"

"I might set up storage in Pomo Bluffs for now and ship the boxes there, if you can coordinate it. Easier than figuring out the East Bay at a distance. What do you think?"

"I'm happy to do that," I said.

Another good-bye. I thought about the timeline. Ylva was dealing with Ansgor. Marget and I needed to try and keep tabs on Galfride, anywhere Ian might go. The Duck 'n Hen, for sure. Near his homes in Pomo Bluffs and the East Bay. Maybe Sophie could suggest more places he frequented.

Thorgisl had gotten through Marget's house protections. That was another concern to be handled.

I had never deliberately courted Bedw. Sophie had strongest tie with her. Bedw had even sensed my son's trouble. Perhaps that was due to her connection with

Sophie; she could have detected my daughter's distress over her brother.

I called Sophie. "Would you consider coming up midweek for a visit?" I asked. I guess my question raised concern.

"Is something wrong?" Sophie wondered.

"No. No. But Rousseau's shipping his things here. We'll need to get them into storage. You could help me set up the guest room for him if you want to." I actually sensed Sophie had the most rapport with the sylphs and wanted to make sure both Marget's and my house were safe but a phone conversation about tightening sylph protections seemed inappropriate.

"As a matter of fact, Ian and I talked about coming up before the weekend. I can be there tomorrow. Most things for school can be done online."

"Are you still loving campus?" I asked.

"Yep. The redwoods and stream, lush lawns and classic buildings haven't gotten old yet."

"That's good. You're not missing Aberystwyth too much??

"Not really. Some things."

"I'd like to hear what when you're here. Oh, could you bring your flute?"

Sophie chuckled. "Sure. Why?"

"I want to hear you play."

"I bet you want Bedw to come for some reason."

Was I mind-speaking with Sophie? "Yeah, maybe. We were scrying and got interrupted by —"

"The Thrizz? We need to find an apt nickname for Galfride. Big G? Maybe Gal-furon," Soph suggested, laughing.

"Oh, that's good. Not exactly shorter though." I joined

her with amused chuckles, which felt good. Worry crept back into my heart. "I've given him a few choice ones from time to time, but I like this best. Maybe just Furon."

"I should start getting ready. Too bad we can't just jump there like you."

"There are downsides—"

"Yeah, yeah. I'll see if Ian wants to drive up tomorrow."

"Bye, sweetie. Be safe."

"You're the one I worry about," she said.

Chapter 8

I found myself pacing. We could scry from my house rather than Marget's. Or try to ask Bedw ourselves right now, so that Marget would be safe. I texted her, asking what she wanted to do, then checked email. A message from Marget popped up.

"Were you trying to reach me?"

I automatically thought-spoke to her rather than type an answer. It was so instantaneous. "I don't like that our scrying was invaded."

"Neither do I."

"I was thinking of asking Bedw to secure your home as she's done for mine."

"Does it keep out EMFs as well?"

I felt her smile. "Maybe so! Though nothing like it existed a thousand years ago. Still. They might adjust quickly. Urban sylphs. But all the toxins for them to filter out might injure them." I hated the thought of their purity tainted.

"I'll check if any are about in the yard. I often spot them." Marget was already on the move.

"You're able to talk with them?"

"Oh, yes."

"I didn't need to get Sophie up here then. Well, I want

to see her anyway. I know she'll enjoy helping get the office ready for Rousseau to stay a bit."

"He's going to live with you?"

"Just until we get him ready to be on his own in the East Bay. Maybe all the threats will be resolved soon. I need to catch you up. I'll wait until you've looked for Bedw, though. I also have something to show you. I finally finished my weaving."

"Sounds thrilling."

Maybe she detected my underlying mood regarding my recent tapestry. "I want your opinion," I said. "Will you come for dinner?"

"I'll be over soon."

While she worked on securing her home, I searched the kitchen for something edible. By the time she appeared at my door, I had tamale pie in the oven and was making salad.

"Bedw is weaving her spells around my home," she said. "I always thought I'd made it safe. I guess my scrying in the attic somehow drew enough attention. But I wonder what could have compromised the roof."

"She'll go up above your house." I remembered standing in the backyard with Baird. It was the first time he called the sylphs.

"She and her cousins," Marget amended. "Still." She had a disconcerted expression. "I always wove sufficient spells in Cornwall."

I thought about saying, "Are you sure?" but decided that was a conversation for another time. "Yes, not just Bedw. We'd better ask Ylva to test it after. Is the breakfast nook okay?" I liked the coziness of it. Besides, the only large table, in the living room, was my work space and would take a lot of clearing.

"Perfect," she said, helping me set the table. "Will you show me now, or after we eat?"

We'd passed through the living room without her noticing the hanging. Now I took her to see my cloth. We stood together, examining it.

"I wish I could see this place in person," she said at last.

"So do I. Though the air is frightening there. I went in spirit travel, to the city, and, I guess because I remembered my son nearly suffocating in that world, I felt I couldn't breathe."

"But the image came to you as you wove."

I nodded. "Ylva had shown me some of it, but there are details past the time she saw it."

"Ylva is amazing, with her dragon worlds and all."

"So are you. That's partly why I wanted to get your opinion. The cloth is already magical, as far as the way it came to be. As if the Stone wove it through my mind. But I'm wondering if I could somehow put a protection spell on it that would keep them safe." I pointed to Shagfen in the shadows. "She's a nyad, or water creature. She's utterly transformed from what we saw in this world."

"You said she was like a bloated toad, right?"

"Exactly. Ylva got her onto Amgath's back and away they flew. Now..." I gestured at the scene by the pool.

Just to be certain, I sent my brand's powers out from my heart to check the perimeters of my home space. Then I said, "I don't want Thorgisl to know where it is, what it looks like. And...I learned the Stone's name."

"It told you?"

"It did. I knew it, when I finished weaving this."

"And you didn't hear Thorgisl in all this time?"

"No. Nothing like when I started it."

"You've learned to secure. I might need your help as well, to put a second layer onto my homestead."

"I'll do my best." I felt the heat of pride rise in my heart. These were powerful people. Not me. How could I have abilities that would help *them*?

After dinner, we played Bananagrams. I beat. "But English is your second language," I apologized.

"You're just good. Tell me your plans for your attic."

I described what we'd worked out and showed her Joaquin's drawings on my computer. Then we climbed the ladder for her to see what we were working with.

"It's going to be marvelous," she said.

Soon after, she left for home.

In bed, I thought about Baird's remark, that he had a ring now that would resonate with mine. I should be able to call to him at any time. Why had I not thought about it until now? A year ago, I'd have thought of nothing else until I used it. To be truthful, it'd been so long since we spent time together that I felt shy.

He hadn't been angry with me, apparently, for running off with Ylva to Jutland without asking for his help, or even his company. He'd been loving. Something else seemed to be niggling at me, making me hesitate.

I longed for our original friendship, the times when we'd shared deeply. I cast my mind back to the start, when I'd looked for him everywhere.

In truth, I felt more involved with Marget and Ylva now. I used to feel I had to go to Aelfwyn for everything. Kyna was the source of my deeper medieval knowledge. Like speaking Middle Welsh. That had been the original seed, but most of our current problems were getting solved with Marget and Ylva.

Boldo had been my go-to for sending messages because

of our tie with the boots. That was sometimes still true. Even Galfride had helped with some emergencies, asked for or not. My son had become entwined in this new configuration.

Baird could not help protect us from Thorgisl and whoever he was aligning with. What if he teamed with the Ronglut? There was that strange scene in Jutland when we'd saved Mora. I knew he wouldn't be above inspiring greed in order to gain strength through force. I still didn't know if the Ronglut had powers, or if Thorgisl brought them magically.

I wondered just how much the dragon might help to quell the Jutland mage's hunger for the Stone. So many questions. I wished I could have daily check-ins with Ylva.

It had happened again; rather than being pulled to contact Baird, I was burning to talk to the Norwegian.

"Ylva? Are you awake?" I asked, gently into the powerful woman's mind, for I never knew what time it might be, with her a thousand years ago.

"I will always wake for you, *félagi*. As it happens, I am gardening. I got ideas from Shelley and Marget in your time and want to try new plants. I have been searching on my travels."

"Ones you can protect from frozen ground?"

"Yes. I will tell you all about it. What worries you?"

"A lot."

"I think Galfride has come back to your time."

I groaned inwardly at the thought of Galfride knowing how to come to my time on his own. Would he stay interested in the 21st century if partnering with Ian did not pan out? Or if Ian went with him to his time? Maybe he'd abandon trying to retrieve the Stone. If that was what he and Thorgisl were cooking up.

"For joy," I said. "What about Ansgor?"

"I have watched him, with little knowing of his aims. I will talk to the idiot today. What else?"

"I'm thinking mostly about Thorgisl. You gave him the dragon—which is growing rapidly. Have you seen?"

Ylva confirmed that she had.

"You said you read the dragon's mind, talked with it? Do you learn from it of Thrizzle's plans? Have you had occasion to influence his thoughts? Is he still in love with it?"

"I believe so. But unfortunately, like any boy with a toy, the initial enchantment has waned so that he is returning to longing for the Stone's power. The parent dragon, Amgath, is forming a strong attachment to the Stone, by the way. You may know how dragons are when they grow fond of an object. She tells me Esch is not, in actuality, amber. It is very ancient, involving plant resins, but not precisely amber."

"I wonder if that would diminish Thorgisl's interest. He does seem obsessed with the qualities of amber."

"It might be information that should be conveyed to the Jutlander," Ylva conceded. "Will you send your son for his next lessons, or come with him?"

"It'll be a few days yet. Otho's the only one who's pulled him to the past, as far as I know, so as long as Otho is contentedly in the tropics…"

"I will check on Otho as well. I will be hopping around the world today."

"Can you do it as you garden?"

"Oh, yes," she said. "I will introduce you to Frigon and we will soon hold council with any who are plotting in regard to Esch."

"Frigon is Amgath's baby?"

She chuckled. "Not so baby now."

"I guess so. He must have grown a lot." I paused, collecting my thoughts. "I especially worry about Thorgisl coming after you. Could he reverse-manipulate? Get his dragon to convince Amgath to bring the Stone to him?"

"You worry too much. This influence will never happen. I assure you, both dragons know what is at stake. Amgath is powerful and clever, and, as I say, attached to Esch."

"I'm sure you know best. I do worry, especially because I feel responsible for your involvement."

I felt her draw up to her full height, and a new emotion—impatience—came through. "You insult me. I have chosen, and fate has chosen, that you be in my spirit-pack. I am not a willy-nilly leaf blown by capricious winds. I decide where and when and how my gifts must and will be used." She stopped her rant.

"I'm sorry. I didn't mean to offend you."

"I love you very much, Kay. We will talk in person soon, and hug."

"I'd like that." I felt meek and chastised as we ended our connection. I had at last pushed her too far. On the other hand, I was glad to know more clearly how she felt.

I curled up and slept, slightly eased by our conversation, though new complications threatened to spiral.

Next day, Sophie arrived in the early afternoon, having dropped off Ian. After a quick lunch—clam chowder, one of her favorites—I asked, "Did you bring your flute?"

"I did. Also, a tin whistle. I'd love to get an old one, I mean ancient."

"I'll ask Boldo. I've heard him play." Was she getting more relaxed about being the only one not to travel to the past? "I'm hoping to see if you can call Bedw by playing it. Just an experiment. She's already bestowed protections on Marget's home and property." I had yet to confirm if that chink in the armor Thorgisl had used to invade our scrying was now patched, but didn't want my daughter feeling I had ulterior motives for her visit.

"Marget invited us over. I thought you'd like to see her garden."

"The rest of her house as well," she said.

"How did it feel, seeing Hamelyn?" I asked. We hadn't talked since then.

"I know you saw us in bed. I felt your presence."

"You seem to be... We've developed some telepathy, you and I," I said.

"Yep."

She was matter-of-fact. It didn't feel like a small thing to me...sharing minds with both of my kids. "It can get sticky at times, I guess,"

"So to speak." She snickered.

"Gross," I said, making a face.

"Goddess," she amended.

"That, too."

"When are we due at Marget's?"

"We can go anytime." This would be my first time to Marget's with just Sophie. "Do you want to unpack or anything?"

"I could. We can look at the den, start setting up for Rousseau. When's his stuff arriving?"

"I'm not sure. Might take a few days. In fact, he might

get here before it does. I'll let Marget know we'll be over in…an hour?"

"That sounds good," Soph said on her way to the den.

"Want a smoothie?"

"That would exactly hit the spot."

We were cleaning up after berry smoothie preparations and consumption when we heard pounding.

Joaquin and a small construction crew were putting up scaffolding on the side of the house.

Sophie raised her brows to me, questioning.

"For the attic," I said. "I'm going to make it bigger, with more ceiling space, and a little balcony at the back."

"Do you think we'll see the sea?" Sophie sounded excited.

"I don't think so. Might be a good time to get out of here, though."

She pressed hands to her ears and nodded agreement.

In minutes, we were out the door, walking toward Marget's. I sent a thought to the Cornish witch, "Do you need anything from the gardens?"

She named six herbs which I recited to Sophie; her memory was far better than mine. But she pulled a small tablet and pen from her backpack to write them down.

"Smart girl."

"No use remembering what you can write, I always say."

"I say that, too," I agreed, giving her a shoulder-nudge. "In my case, it's pretty much necessary all the time."

"You just have too much packed into your head," she said, nudging me back.

Chapter 9

At Shelley's plot, I said, "Now it's a matter of identifying them."

"Got my phone." Sophie pulled it from a pocket. "We can look them up."

"The ones that aren't labeled. But she's pretty thorough about that."

For the next half hour, we searched for her neat signs with herb names, found four of the ones we needed, looked up the other two and identified them.

With tufts of each tucked into the backpack, we walked on to Marget's. I took Sophie's hand at the fence. We waited for a man to walk his dog out of the park before "jumping" to the other side.

"How does she get deliveries?" Sophie asked.

"I don't think she gets many. But knowing her, she can probably manifest a gate when needed."

"It must confuse the meter man to see that decrepit house in the front and then—whoa." She became entranced with the sweet paths bursting with carefully tended herbs and flowering vines.

"Mom, we have to make your yard look like this! Bedw and her sisters would love it." She sniffed flowers and touched leaves of a wide variety. "Did you say she brought plants from ancient Cornwall?"

The back door opened.

"Your cultivation is being appreciated," I said.

Marget descended the several stairs and joined Sophie beside a flowering plant that looked like a snapdragon. "Toadflax," she said. "*Linaria vulgaris.*"

"You know the Latin for all of these?" Sophie sounded impressed.

"Would you like to learn?" She put an arm around Sophie's waist, smiling up at her.

"She has a great mind for details," I said. "Hey, Soph, I bet the lore around old plants would go well with your major."

"Definitely. I'll see if I can work in research on that with my advisor. There are probably songs associated with many of these?"

"Are there ever!" Marget smiled. "Endless songs based on plants." She touched a branch and sang about the willow. Moving around the garden, she crooned half a dozen other tunes.

I contributed, "The bonnie, bonnie broom o' th' Cowdeknowes."

"A Scottish tune. I do love the sight o' broom," she said. "Though I don't dare bring it here. There's such a stink about its invasiveness."

I laughed. "I know. Fire concerns. It's a crime to mention deer fondly because they eat people's plants. Very anthropocentric."

"How do you know that song, Mom?"

"I don't know. Maybe Kyna."

Sophie had her notebook out and had been writing madly. "This is heather, isn't it? What did you call it?"

"*Grig.* Child, I could do this for hours. Are you hungry, though?"

"We had a smoothie at Mom's when I arrived so—"

"What would you like to do first, then?" Marget asked, clearly taken with my daughter's enthusiasm.

Sophie rummaged in her backpack and pulled out her flute and phone. She assembled the silver flute, inherited from her great-grandfather. Then she set her phone to record. "Will you teach me one song? I'll record it and practice."

The three of us sat at the small table in the bower, where Rousseau had recently joined us.

Marget chose *Du ha'n Owr*. "When the *furse* be out o' blossom, kissin's out o' fashion."

At the end, Sophie clapped, then said, laughing, "That's because it's always in bloom, right?"

"You be correct, child." Marget's face crinkled in a smile.

"Could you sing the first line again?" Sophie played the notes, following after Marget.

As they worked back and forth, I wandered through the garden, listening. This was a restful and rewarding time. I savored it, letting worries dissolve.

When Sophie was satisfied that she had enough to go on for learning the song and understanding its meaning— she wrote the words and translation as well—we went inside.

"I'd like to see the other parts of your house," Sophie said to Marget. "Rousseau told me about the living room, and the sewing/writing room, and especially the attic. Oh! Look at this kitchen. It's like a past era."

"I've tended to accouter it with what I know."

"You can get secondhand things online that are pretty old-fashioned," Sophie suggested, "if you need to. But…not a thousand years old."

Marget laughed. "I think I might have enough, but I'll keep that in mind."

Sophie traipsed into the living room, gawked at the misty center that obscured the street side. "Spooky," she said, glancing into a dining room I'd not known of. Then she hurried up the stairs. She stopped mid-way. "Is it okay?"

"Yes, girl. Go where you please."

"Where's your bedroom?" she called over her shoulder.

"Soph!" I glanced an apology to Marget.

"Don't worry. She's fine." She called up the stairwell, "It's to your left, at the top."

We heard Sophie's footsteps whirl through the bedroom, then into the sitting room. "This is divine. You can look out at the park while you work. I'd love a room like this."

I immediately wanted a second story, not just an expanded attic.

"But your house is great, too, Mom," she called. Either the telepathy continued or she was just being incredibly astute. "Did you know she's adding more space to the attic?" Sophie called down to Marget as she started toward the third stairway.

"I did hear about that," Marget said, chuckling.

We'd reached the first landing.

"She wants to be more like you."

Sophie stopped. "Is it okay for me to go to your magical room?"

"Certainly, dear. You keep right on up."

We joined her in the mysterious, peak-roofed attic that enthralled my son. Sophie moved around from altar to curtained scrying area, then stood by the narrow window that looked out the back. She opened drawers in the scroll-top desk, then turned to study the opposite wall that faced the street. It had only one small round window at the top.

"Do you try to make sure no one can see the house from the street side?" Sophie asked.

"I suspect it's invisible to most people, but we should probably test that theory."

"Did Bedw secure it all?" I asked.

"Want to check now?"

"Yes." I sat on one of her thick round pillows—probably from the meditation store downtown. Cross-legged, hands rested in my lap, rings touching, I constellated my brand, sending energy from my heart.

Above the house, I directed feelers along the roof line. Dread sank into my heart when I encountered a hitch, a dark place I'd never experienced before. I explored, circling its icy nothingness, having no idea how to remove it.

Bringing my senses back into the room, I scrambled to my feet and dashed downstairs, Marget and Sophie on my heels with worried faces.

"What is it?" Marget called as we ran.

In the garden, I dropped to my knees on a clover patch and crawled to where I'd seen Bedw weeks before. Or was it days?

Sophie knelt next to me. She seemed to anticipate my intention for she held the tin whistle. But we didn't need it; Marget settled beside us and we hummed a note, first in our minds. It felt right.

Slowly, I made out a swarm of moving dots among the leaves. I picked out Bedw's shades of green and brown. There were sky blue and indigo, rust and gold, plum and violet. I had never made requests to sylphs myself. Not knowing their language, I searched within and let Kyna's knowledge come forth, then sent a mind-message on a frequency I'd never used. Again, it felt right. "When you were making Marget's home safe, did you find something on the roof? Something—" I gave a mental-message of the feeling it had given me— "malevolent?"

Bedw moved toward me. I heard a burring, trilling sound, and thought I caught an affirmative answer.

"Have you ever found that before?" I asked.

"Never." I thought that was her message.

"I need to ask Ylva," I said to Marget.

I perceived my heron-spirit, at the far edge of the garden, in shadow. I wasn't sure if the others saw her. I thought toward her, "I've found…badness, above Marget's house." I still did not have a strong sense of how to communicate with her. I slipped my hand onto the heron-stone in my pocket.

With heart-stopping grace, she unfolded wide wings and flew up over the roof. My heart gripped with fear that she might be hurt, flying through that place.

A minute later, Ylva stood in the garden. Sophie jumped.

"Did my hegri call you here?" I asked. My spirit-bird had helped me before, in Thorgisl's fort, even when I had no memory of any of them, so she must always sense my need.

Ylva nodded. "She told my wolf. Now you shall all see," she said mysteriously, and waved toward the sky.

We watched above, hands shading out a glary half-overcast sun, as an immense dragon flew from the east. Semi-translucent, with coruscating iridescent colors, it swept over the house. A dark rain crackled above the roof, making rustling, snapping sounds. A dark smoky shape rose, vertical, like a twister.

The dragon circled and swept down again toward the roof. Again, crackling flickers snapped, like electricity, and shot in spurts above the house. I smelled a stink of burning tar. This time the insidious darkness writhed, and dispersed. A residue lingered, but a third onslaught by the dragon annihilated the last wisp.

Hegri launched from a high perch and winged over the house. Bedw and her sisters also fluttered up moving in patterns above the roof.

It was a sight to behold, our own Aurora Borealis.

Then the dragon was nowhere to be seen. My heron landed again in the shadows of the yard. As the sylphs drifted down, I asked the Otherworld beings, "Is it safe now?"

Unable to discern a response, I turned to Ylva.

"It was hard to detect, I imagine," Ylva said. "Galfride probably opened a breach from inside the attic room."

My mouth dropped open. Any softening I'd felt—any bit of trust that had formed—disintegrated into rage.

"I hate that man." Marget's expression mirrored my emotions.

"He will do anything to get an edge on re-establishing contact with Ian," I said. "Do you think that's all it is?"

"It is not Galfride. It is Thorgisl, using Galfride," Ylva stated. "I taste magic. Everyone's is distinct. Galfride's has a very different...hm, aura. He manipulates minds. And amasses fine things because they please him. A few have uses but most have an aesthetic he likes. Thorgisl, on the other hand, is obsessed that someone might gain a power he lacks, through objects." She turned to me. "You've been in his mind. You know all this."

"He shows me clean sterile hallways of his mind, nothing more. I have no ability to go deeper, like you and Aelfwyn can."

"I'd think he'd put his efforts toward Ylva for that," Marget said.

"He'd never have the nerve." Ylva sounded dismissive.

"He was in your home," I mentioned in a low voice, hoping I wouldn't raise the big woman's ire.

"Galfride, you mean? My home is safe, inviolable," she assured us.

"You do have the dragons," I said.

Sophie sat by the ferns the sylphs loved best, and quietly played a melodic Celtic tune on the tin whistle. I thought it might be a thanks. They vibrated fast with a subtle hum, blending into one another, separating and blending again. I was certain they gave my daughter messages. She smiled and sang-spoke to them.

Ylva remarked, "Finding out about the Stone is Thorgisl's obsession. Ian is Galfride's. But Thorgisl would use any of Galfride's passions to gain access to you. He might hope to reach me through you, gain information."

Marget and I looked at each other.

"And he breached Marget's home rather than mine," I said, rhetorically.

"Has Galfride been in your home?" Ylva asked.

I pondered. "No, I don't think he ever has. "That's a sickening thought. We have to somehow—"

"—influence them away from the Stone. I agree." Ylva fingered a leaf thoughtfully.

"Give them something else to think about? You'd hoped the dragon would do that," I said, disheartened.

"I never thought it was a permanent solution. I also hadn't figured on this new alliance."

Chapter 10

I sent my sphere of protection, just to make sure we were unheard, out around Marget's yard. "Do you think Galfride is telling Ansgor about the power of the Stone, to try to get him to team with them?"

"Since they can't go to Sartren themselves—"

"Is that the name of the other planet, or dimension?"

"I believe so. Therefore, they're likely trying to overpower me to get it for them."

"Do you think they know you've sent the Stone there?" I asked.

"Didn't you say Galfride knew?"

"He seemed to. He must have been listening through his breach in the roof," I said, nauseated. "We thought we'd been so careful. It's truly bad if Thorgisl knows."

"As you've suggested, Kay, they might try to find a soft spot of mine," said Ylva. "Like you, my folk, the dragons. I love too much."

"Me." I felt light headed. I was a soft spot of hers? I made her vulnerable?

"They know my fondnesses. I'll do anything to save you, or any of my spirit-clan. Therefore, all you love matters to me as well and must be protected. But I have great strength and a vast ability to protect."

"They might try to hold hostages to make you bring them Esch," I said, remembering how long Thorgisl held me, tearing away my memories of all I held dear, before I was saved, how long he hid Boldo, and Mora, both suffering terribly. Ylva felt herself invulnerable but it wasn't quite true.

"I didn't know you so well then, *nipt*."

I felt bad that Ylva had sensed my thoughts, but she may as well know my concerns.

"More training," Ylva said. "Without delay. So we can all detect such violations right away.

I nodded, happy to have an aim. "Hopefully you taught Rousseau enough that he can make it here safely."

"Do you know when he arrives?"

"Friday," I said.

"I will guard over him," she said, "and will ask your hegri to watch closely over you."

We climbed to the attic room. This time no insidious, inky barrier hovered above.

"If I scry, there should be no invasion, no prying." Marget looked from me to Ylva.

"There should not." Ylva, standing near the altar, perused the contents with interest. She turned to us. "I want to plan our next steps. Maybe we should do it with The Thirteen, to add weight. On the other hand, maybe the three of us need to meet with Thorgisl, Galfride, and whoever else they're canoodling with first." She turned to Marget. "This will be a good space. I feel sure the dragon, Triloss, left more protections than the sylphs over your home, though their magic is splendid in all regards, bestowing good feelings." She put her large hands on Marget's small shoulders. "This must be most distressing for you. Shall we go down to the kitchen and drink tea?"

"Let's do." Marget seemed affected by Ylva's energy as she lifted her strong hands away.

We descended the stairs. Soon there was a cozy fire crackling in the wood burning stove. Marget prepared an aromatic tea, with lavender and fennel flavor.

I called in Sophie. She delighted over Marget's cup collection before picking one covered with hummingbirds.

Ylva dominated the table, backing up to fit her legs under. We sipped companionably for a time.

Marget fetched shortbread cookies. We spent time talking about things not involving danger.

Sophie described her major. "It combines folklore, music, and linguistics," she explained.

Marget and Ylva appeared to make an effort taking this in.

"You'll have to tell us what you come up with," Ylva said.

Sophie laughed. "I'm sure I'll be able to tell you something."

"Darling, I have a set of scenes you might enjoy, upstairs. Would you like to explore?"

Sophie brightened. "I'd love to."

I figured she was getting her out of the room so we could plan. Some of it could be distressing.

When Marget came downstairs alone, Ylva told us, "I have a special kind of silent sphere. Your daughter will still hear our voices but will not understand words or thoughts."

"I'd like to learn that one," I said.

"I will teach you." She folded her hands on the table, looking ready to parley.

"So, you think we should talk to Thorgisl?" I asked. "If so, with what bargaining tool?"

"I will communicate first, perhaps with the scrying bowl, attempting to convince him that going after the Stone is futile. It will always make its way back to its mountain."

"Do we know if he can get to Sartren?" I asked. "We need a way to listen and read his thoughts."

"I have access, through Frigon."

I thought about it. "What if Thorgisl detects that Frigon is your messenger, your spy? Maybe Esch has ideas." I had to admit, I wanted to have contact with the Stone again. I wanted to feel that overpowering sense of love.

"That is a good thought," Ylva agreed.

"Is there some way…" I trailed off, knowing it would be foolhardy to return to that world where I could not breathe. "That priestess said she made the air worse for the men on the ship. Maybe it's breathable in the mountains." I could also go in spirit. But I longed to put my hand on the Stone. I had to ask myself: Was I being drawn?

"We can go in spirit and talk with it." Ylva squinted at me and I knew she'd caught some of my thoughts.

"Could I go, too?" Marget asked.

"We can try." Ylva put her hand on Marget's. "I would like to solve the issues around your son and Galfride as well."

Marget nodded.

Ylva turned to me. "And what about your daughter? Should we try to see what hampers her time travel?"

My heart sagged. Truth be told, I'd preferred only worrying about Rousseau being pulled to that time, or encountering the trouble that could occur there. Now Sophie was of interest due to her connection to Ian. This issue couldn't be avoided forever. And I knew it wasn't fair to not ask her how she felt. "Should we wait until…"

"We should not wait. I do not think waiting is wise. She and Rousseau both need to be able to protect themselves." Ylva emptied her cup. "What if she's pulled and harmed?"

I felt pressured. Rousseau would arrive Friday. It was now Wednesday. "He's coming here in two days. We could focus on getting him trained."

"Two days." Ylva leveled me with a steady gaze. "Lots could happen in that amount of time. I cannot protect him in Bot-son and all points in between as well as I can here, or on my mountain."

Sophie snickered from the doorway. "Boston," she whispered. She had come downstairs and stood in the doorway, unnoticed until she spoke.

"Boss-ton," Ylva amended with exaggeration. "I take him to the mountain. My people keep him safe. I check over Sophie and leave her safely here with Marget. Then we all join together on Galdhøpiggen."

"Alright," I said. Staring down into my tea, I spoke to Rousseau. I found no one. I looked in horror at the others around the table. "I don't feel his mind!"

Sophie sat at the table. "Can you always feel him if you try?"

"Always." My throat strangled on the word.

Marget stood. "Let's don't panic. We'll scry his apartment, go there if we need to."

In her attic room, we hunched over the scrying bowl. Marget brought his apartment into view. Ylva sat very still. I assumed she was already there. I joined her spirit.

We walked through the empty apartment. It was cleared out, boxes gone. No Rousseau.

We re-entered our bodies in Marget's attic room.

Ylva sat cross-legged, holding a small carven wolf.

After a long moment, she said, "He does not appear in the air or on the water, this time or ours. We try Thrizzle's tower." She kept an even tone as I barely held back full panic.

Sophie sat, shoulder pressed to mine, watching the water and our faces.

This time I shot out in spirit with Ylva, as she examined Thorgisl's tower room; he stood fiddling with a strange, dark object, perhaps carved obsidian. Ylva slipped into his mind, carrying me along. I gasped, in spirit, at the sheer gall. This was a man of consummate mind-power, but Ylva had shunted us down to the most miniscule of vibrations, perhaps a spider. We slipped through swiftly to find out if he kept my son hostage somewhere in the fort.

The Jutland mage sat down by the long tower window and stared out. He watched Frigon flying out over the sea. The dragon was about half his adult size now. He made himself invisible to anyone but a few.

"I know you're there," Thorgisl said to us. "It's impolite to jump into another's mind, as when you leapt— The Thirteen—into my tower room and took the stone I had purchased."

"Kay's son is missing," Ylva said to him. "Do you know anything about that?"

Thorgisl gave a great heaving, bored sigh. "I have nothing to do with any disappearance of the lad. But I have many thoughts about havoc I can wreak on your people if you don't give me back my Stone."

We appeared outside of him. It was too uncomfortable to try to dwell in his mind and communicate with him at the same time, especially when he was angry. He had also put up walls around us, creating a bare cell in his mind. I'd spent many hours in cells of his creation as his captive. My heart quelled at being there again.

"The Stone—Esch—is where it wants to be," I said, now standing in spirit form outside of him in his tower room.

"So, you do know where it is?" Thorgisl made a move to trap me but Ylsa held him still with a look.

"Do you not see that Esch has sentience and is not to be owned, or brought to our world, away from the world it loves?" she asked.

He sat frozen, except for his lips which could unfortunately still spew forth words. "The amber told you all this, did it?" he sneered.

"Oh, yes. And it's not amber, by the way," I said.

His brow flickered in surprise.

"You have many powerful ambers. You have a dragon now. Why do you need this otherworld stone?"

Ylva had settled in one of his hammock chairs, at least visually. Her spirit could be anywhere. She would arrange herself to have the most influence. She gave him a picture of Esch, not where it was, but how it felt.

Was it wise, I wondered, to give him even that? Could the sensations help him find the Stone? I feared angering him. What might he do to Frigon in order to manipulate us?

Thorgisl moved, stretched, twisted his head as if uncomfortable. Ylva must have released her tether on him, but I felt her monitoring his every muscle. "What do you offer me, Giantess? Are you in league with the Ice Giants?"

That surprised her. I felt it though she did not show it. "That depends on what you want ultimately," she responded.

"What I want, ultimately." He gave a cold laugh.

"For what do you amass power?" she asked. "Merely

to grow stronger? To acquire more baubles? When will it be enough?"

"Oh yes. I have so much. Traveling with filthy, foul-mouthed louts. Making sure they have—" Thorgisl stopped. "I have no need to reveal my motivations and dreams to you. Give me some incentive to leave the stone you call Esch." He pronounced the name I loved with sarcasm, making me bristle.

Ylva asked, "Do you know what Sartren is like? There is too little oxygen for humans. Far off in the remotest part, Esch has beauty. But in the populated areas, there are despots, fathers who sell their nyad daughters into slavery. That may not trouble you, nor the fact that Otho and his men would be tried for theft if found in that world."

"Why should it?" Thorgisl said petulantly.

I couldn't read his stiff face. I'd draped my spirit self into another of the hammock chairs facing him.

"Perhaps you'd enjoy a world like that, if you could manage the air." Ylva ribbed him, exploring.

"I don't propose moving there. Only getting the power stone back. Maybe there are more like it that aren't so choosy about locale." He smirked.

"What do you need this further power for?"

"To influence minds. Make them malleable. Of course. How is it not clear, such a desire?" He seemed genuinely puzzled.

I thought of Galfride, and how similar their addictions were, in this sense. But did they really coincide?

"What for?" Ylva asked. "What do you want people to do? Do you work for someone who desires to gain lands? What does he, or she, hold over you?"

"Do you know there are constant incursions into our lands?" he asked. "The Danes. The Romans. Your people."

"But capturing Boldo, Kay, and Mora. These were not about invaders of Jutland."

"As you now know, I was still trying to get the Stone. Esch as you call it. Track down Otho who'd disappeared with it."

"He and his ship were caught in a time warp before they ended up on Sartren. Did you know that?"

Thorgisl looked interested.

Was a time warp something else he thought he might exploit?

"When did you learn of this?" he asked.

I actually wondered the same thing. Had my son been caught in the time warp as well?

Ylva ignored his question. "You want Esch to help you repulse invaders." She tried to piece the together reasoning.

"Might." He looked decidedly crafty now.

"Are you forming an alliance with Galfride and Ansgor?" I asked. "The Ronglut?"

Thorgisl sputtered a laugh. "The Ronglut? Good god, no. What do they have for me? I trust them less than a hangnail." He paused. "Galfride tried. Came to me wanting my help with this sad little toady. What's his name, Ian?"

I cringed, hoping Marget hadn't followed along for any of this conversation.

"He even offered to help obtain Esch, which, now I know it's not amber, I may have lost some of my appetite anyway. Yes, he suggested Ansgor might bring his inimitable talents. I know of the Saxon." He flipped a dismissive hand.

"So, he had nothing of interest to offer you?" Ylva asked.

I watched the exchange with growing dread. Where would this lead?

Ylva stretched her long frame as though there in the flesh. "How about if you be straight with me. What are you considering doing in order to gain the stone—which is not, by the way, ownable. And since that world does not make amber, it likely does not have the powers you desire."

"Still has power." Thorgisl recrossed his legs, seeming to enjoy the cat-and-mouse game in which they engaged. "Maybe more than ancient amber." He was truly enamored. But in what? His perception of the stone.

I had the detected shock in his body-language, though, upon learning it was not amber, as he'd clearly assumed it was for a very long time.

"Still has power. Maybe more than ancient amber."

He was truly enamored. But in what? His perception of the stone.

"It pulled an entire ship into a time warp and thence onto its home planet. Or we assume it to be, at any rate."

I thought he could be blustering his way through an all-out inner meltdown.

"And what is the stone's constitution then? Something with a conscience, a mind." There was skepticism etched on his face, yet I felt a new curiosity growing in him. "Never mind. Are you able to find power stones in this world? I've heard that Duff can. Isn't he your lover?"

A lightning bolt shot through Ylva at his mention of the man she adored. She had it entirely under control, as far as anyone else could detect, but her broiling emotions were like a bubbling cauldron. Still, her mind worked with its usual clever discernment, clear despite the uproar. Or merely energized to the full degree. "My Duff is a talented man," she said, "who is under my protection."

"And that is a daunting thing." Thorgisl gave his sardonic smile. "However, we might be able to strike a deal."

"I thought you didn't have Rousseau. Or know anything about his disappearance," she said.

"I don't. I speak of your desire for me to forget about Esch."

"You forget I have no desire to help empower you, with new stones or otherwise," she said.

"Must we be at odds? You never know what trouble I might wreak on Kay's friends, her children. Or *your* kin for that matter. I can be all manner of disruptive."

"Now you are focused on Duff's talent with stones?" she asked as if reprimanding a toddler who'd discovered breaking things as a pastime.

"A truce, for now," he proposed. "My taste for power remains as ever, but at the moment, I do enjoy my dragon gift from you." He swept an arm toward the window opening.

"As long as you don't use him for dominance or destruction," Ylva said.

"Are you saying you would consider taking him back?" he asked. "Now that *would* be a mistake."

"I'm saying I know his kin. And he is not to be used in harmful ways."

"Why would you give him to such as me, then?" he asked, all wide-eyed curiosity.

"I thought even you could change, in the presence of such a mind as his."

"Don't pretend to read me, witch." Thorgisl stood abruptly. Clearly he did not like the hint of manipulation. "I change for no one."

She stood at her full height and looked down at him. "A truce, then, meaning no abductions on your part while Frigon remains with you? Or what?"

"Do you trust my word, Great Shamaness of the *Galdhøpiggen Mountain*?"

"Trust. It is a complex concept," Ylva said. "I believe we need to hold values of equal measure in our hearts."

"I wish to speak more of the Ice Giants," Thorgisl stated.

I had never seen the demeanor of honest interest and respect he showed now. Of course, he seemed to be able to manufacture any expression, but I perceived him, at that moment, through Ylva's discerning eye.

"We will speak more then," she said. And for a moment, she stepped into him. An exchange occurred of such depth, I could not follow, then we were gone.

Chapter 11

Back at Marget's, I asked, "Do you believe him? That he turned down Galfride's offers, and knows nothing of my son's disappearance?" I was near tears, wringing my hands.

"Thrizzle thinks he has barriers to me. He has none. He does not have Rousseau, and has had very little contact with Galfride. He scoffed. He has little respect for Galfride, thinks he has small talent and fiddles with silly gadgets."

"You're pretty sure about Otho being contented in the South Seas? He's the one who's pulled Rousseau away before."

"Yes, I'm sure about Otho."

Marget asked, "What happened?"

"His interests leap from one thing to another."

"What have they leapt to?" Marget asked.

I paced the room. "We need to find Galfride."

Marget and Ylva scryed, searching for the man, and then Ian. Not locating the former, they found Ian easily enough at a café in town. He was playing his mandolin softly, scribbling a song on a notepad.

"Galfride must be close by," I said.

"Mayhap he uses those gadgets to hide himself. They're not something with which I'm acquainted." Ylva seemed uncomfortable with this mystery.

Sophie yawned and a tear squeezed out, rolling down her cheek.

I hugged her. "Let's try to get some sleep."

"I go home, too," Ylva said. "But I watch and I tell you."

We hugged Marget. "You get rest, too. At least Ian seems fine," I said.

I transported Sophie and I to our home where we sat in the living room. I'd never done that before—transported from her house to ours, definitely not with my daughter.

"You're getting really magical," Sophie mumbled, head buried in my shoulder. She seemed to have no trouble with being transported in our time.

"We didn't leave Marget too abruptly, did we?" I asked.

"It feels like it, when you get from one place to another so quickly," Sophie said, still in awe.

We noticed Rousseau's luggage near the doorway to the guest room.

Sophie gave a sobbing cry. "Rousseau?" She ran into the den.

I followed close behind. We looked around. My son was not there. We dashed through the house calling. I grabbed my phone and texted him. No reply. We looked at each other.

"I hate this!" Sophie wailed.

"Let's each have a hot bath," I coaxed. There was little we could do, except wait for one of our powerful witch friends to find him. I started a bath, feeling filled with dread.

Sophie trailed behind me. I got her to climb into the bath first.

While she soaked, I made cocoa-carob drink with honey

and goat milk with a touch of pepper and cinnamon the way she loved it, and brought it to her. She sipped, lids swollen and red.

I lay on my bed, making myself breathe slowly, and pressing the rings to the silver as I constellated my brand. This time, as I touched each sigil with my mind, I thought of my hegri, forming the heron's image in my mind. I felt her just outside the house—she rarely came into enclosed spaces.

"No one can find my son," I thought to her. "No use calling Ylva. She's already tried. We can't find Galfride, either." I felt for her, trying to explore if she knew Rousseau's energy.

She sent back a clear image of my son who appeared safe. I thanked her. As we moved this intense energy back and forth, Bedw took shape outside the window, fluttering. As always, her sweet tune helped my heart, this time just a little. There were other sylphs with her. I realized I was humming the note we'd sung together earlier in the day. Then I heard Sophie, in the bath, join. Even Hegri seemed to intone it in small cries.

My daughter emerged wrapped in a robe. "They're going to look for him, I think." She snuggled next to me on the bed. "Was that your spirit-heron singing with us?"

Communication with these fae beings seemed to come naturally to her.

I skipped my bath, feeling like I needed to keep comforting my daughter. I changed into my nightgown and we snuggled up with books on my bed. She wasn't the only one comforted.

I didn't think I could possibly sleep, but woke from a dream. I was in the narrow cave alcove, curled around Esch. The stone, at my belly, sent that same powerful love vibration, the dream-sense of being known fully, a knowing I've rarely perceived in waking life. The sylphs were there with us, in that other world, whirling and circling with huge butterflies.

Suddenly I stood in front of Marget's shed, in her abandoned front yard. The sylphs hovered near me.

I saw through the wall of Marget's shed. Rousseau sat on an old plastic chair, focus glazed over as I'd seen Gwynedd years before, in Galfride's cave.

Behind me, Galfride said, "I will not release him until your daughter lets go of her hold on Ian."

I gasped, wanting to do harm to him.

I woke with a start, in my bed. Had it been real, a true answer? I ran for my cape and, as I pulled on sweats and boots, called to Ylva, then Marget. I sent myself to the shed. Both women met me there. I relayed the dream in short bursts as I fumbled with the latch on the door. Ylva burst it open with a flash from her palm.

There sat my son, untied but unmoving. I hated seeing that blind stare, and rushed to him, wrapping my arms around him.

"We need to get Aelfwyn and Kyna here," I said. "That's how we broke this spell the last time, with Gwynedd." I called to them, my brand constellated and felt them immediately, but also saw Galfride in the shadows outside the door of the shed.

"Won't be so easy this time," he said, walking toward me.

"Easy?" I hissed, astounded.

"How did ye find me?"

"Like I'd tell you. Why are you doing this?"

"I thought you'd know." He looked at me strangely.

Was in my dream? I hoped he wasn't able to do that, but wouldn't be surprised.

"Your daughter be keepin' Ian from me. I want her out o' the picture."

"And then you'll release my son?" I asked.

Ylva stared at me, then turned to Galfride. "She'll make no such promise."

What did he mean by my daughter out of the picture. I'd assumed he'd never hurt Sophie, no matter how much he resented her place in Ian's affections, because that wouldn't be any way to regain Ian's friendship.

Aelfwyn and Kyna walked into the shed. "Not as easy?" Kyna asked, all spite. "I had almost hoped you'd got past this childish means o' garnerin' attention."

Kyna, Aelfwyn, and I built the lightning bolt that had shattered the shield before. Nothing changed. Galfride laughed.

I searched and found tiny beams of light coming from the corners of the shed. Just as Ylva had suspected. "You bastard. I thought you were Rousseau's friend."

A red bolt shot out of Ylva's pocket. A small fiery dragon swept around the building several times.

Rousseau's head lifted, fully focused on me. I cried out and threw my arms around him.

"You'd better not have wrecked my instruments," Galfride snarled, glaring at the winged salamander, and rushing to a corner.

"I may not know about gadgets," Ylva said. "But *xharzers* figure things out quickly."

Rousseau stepped toward Galfride. "That was despicable."

"Sorry, mate. Was runnin' out o' options." Galfride stared at a device in his hand. He put out his other hand as if to shake.

Rousseau smacked it away and strode from the shed,

ducking under the doorjamb.

"What are we gonna do with you?" Ylva tsked down at Galfride. "Whatever we think of, it's gonna hurt, scamp."

"That's to say it lightly," Aelfwyn snapped. "What do you say we imprison him for a bit, give him a taste of his medicine."

Before he could disappear, Ylva had him in a jar the size of her thumb. "I'll keep him with me. We can talk terms later."

We heard a tiny voice, yelling.

Rousseau cracked a half smile.

I took his hand. "Thank you, everyone." Blowing kisses all around, I left with my son.

We appeared in our front hall.

"You're getting good at that." He gave me a wrap-around hug. We stayed that way a long moment. "I could have saved my plane fare." He chuckled though he was clearly not yet over the ordeal.

I gave a shaky answering laugh that was filled with relief, as well as exhaustion and a residue of fear.

"Sophie's going to be happy. She was really upset."

"She's here?"

"Yep." I led him to my room.

He ruffled her curls softly, more affectionate than usual—maybe due to his close call, and knowing she'd been upset for him.

"Mom?" Sophie croaked. She flipped on the light and turned.

Rousseau chuckled as she sat bolt upright, then jumped onto the bed to throw herself at him

"You're here." On a sob, she mumbled, "This has to stop," and stomped her bare foot.

"I agree." He hugged her back.

"What do you need? Shower? Food?" I asked.

"Food would be great. Water."

I brought him cold water and hurried to make an egg scramble. "I can't believe you were out there while we were inside Marget's house, then off to ancient Jutland looking for you. Tell us what happened. We saw your luggage a little while ago."

He helped himself to more spring water from the fridge. "I was going to surprise you. I took an Airporter to the shuttle, and grabbed an Uber here. I'd just gotten in when I found myself in that shed and couldn't move."

"What time did you arrive?" I asked.

"Like, three o'clock?"

"So, we were at Marget's, absorbed with getting Galfride's odious spy-cloud off the roof. He's become our biggest worry, with his obsession over Ian. We went and talked to Thrizzle, in our search for you."

"You what? Mom, I don't want you putting yourself in danger over me."

Chapter 12

W hat else would I do? You wouldn't be involved in any of this if it weren't for me."

"I'm not sure that's true, Mom. Baird appeared to me on the subway. Maybe it was just chance that they found you first." I started to respond but he went on. "Wasn't that the same as the spell on Gwynedd? When I heard her screaming and she came into your dream?"

"Right. But this time we weren't able to break the spell."

"He's done something more to his gadgets since then."

"What a despicable use of his talents," I said, bringing Rousseau a chocolate drink.

Sophie joined us, wrapped in a warm robe.

"Did you learn anything from Thorgisl?" he asked.

"The Thrizz?" Sophie said the name with venom. She had cause to hate him. He'd threatened her family.

"Do you think he's teaming with Galfride?" Rousseau went on.

I tried to reassure them. "I feel an inkling of hope that Ylva may distract him from the Stone, which could mean away from us. I'm frustrated, though, that you were just feet away and we couldn't sense you. Even Marget and Ylva couldn't. He hid you with those instruments." I scowled, a bitter taste in my mouth. He'd used them for good at the Brocken when he first showed us Ansgor, and Ylva. But now, this!

Sophie rubbed sleepy eyes, sitting in the kitchen alcove. "I can't believe he'd do that. Did he say why?"

"He sees you as a barrier to getting Ian back," I said.

"What is it they have, some kind of bromance?" Sophie got up to search for coffee.

I said, "I'm not sure about that. I only know they were close in their teens. Ian was younger, maybe twelve. I think Galfride has been lonely. He used to seek out Kyna as a partner. Then he wanted me to help him get to his biological son, Hamelyn."

At the name of her former love, Sophie jerked the carafe she was sniffing for freshness, spilling some. Then she nodded, remembering Galfride, not Baird, had sired Hamelyn.

I went on, "Now he sees Ian as an old mate, someone who shared his passion for magic, I suppose."

"What happened? I'm going to make herb tea." She set down the cold coffee and put on water to boil.

"Ylva took him away in a tiny jar," Rousseau said, scraping up the last of his eggs with toast.

"For real?" Sophie looked dumbfounded. "How long will she keep him like that?"

"Good question." I laughed.

"He deserves it anyway," Sophie fumed, waiting for the water to boil.

"It's about time he got the captivity treatment," Rousseau said, still angry. "Have some scramble if you're hungry." He pointed to the pan.

Soph shook her head. "Did the sylphs help you find him?" she asked me.

"Yes. They came to me in a dream and showed me the shed. Galfride said in the dream almost the same thing as he said for real at Marget's shed."

"That you needed to make me stay away from Ian or he'd keep taking Rousseau captive? That's so…creepy." She changed her mind and scooped eggs onto a plate, then brought them to the table with her tea.

"First, in the dream, I was in the grotto, curled up to Esch. I think I told him in the dream about Rousseau's disappearance." I stopped. "I don't know why I call the stone 'him'. Anyway, then I was standing in front of the shed and could see Rousseau inside, through the wall." I pressed my shoulder to him, just to feel his warmth and solidity. "I woke up and went there."

"Why didn't you get me up?" Sophie wants to know.

I took her hand across the table. "You were sleeping. I wasn't sure. So, I decided to just bring him back if I could."

"You've put together a pretty great team," Rousseau said. "And you're pretty bad-ass yourself. What do we do now?"

"Get you more training."

"When they let Galfride out," Sophie said before biting into toast, "he'll be so mad and I'm sure he won't have forgotten Ian."

"Maybe Ylva can talk sense into him," I suggested, with more hope than assurance.

"What about Ansgor? Wasn't he the one behind Galfride trying to get Kyna? And Gwynedd?"

"Galfride has spoken with him, and suggested alliance between him and Thorgisl. Ylva said she'll talk to him today. I don't know if she's gotten around to it. I keep calling her for other emergencies. She hardly gets a chance."

"You said something about Marget's roof?" Rousseau said. "That was the first emergency?"

"It was so cool," Sophie said with wonder.

I thought she was glad to have been part of something. "Ylva called a dragon."

"I think we'll need to fill you in with the rest tomorrow," I said with a yawn. "You must be tired. The bed's ready."

We walked to the den.

"You're the tired one, Mom." He flopped onto the office fold-out that luckily had clean sheets.

"Good-night." I kissed his forehead.

He was already pulling out his laptop. "Night, Mom. Thanks for saving me."

Instead of feeling pleased, guilt coursed through me for his recent experience with Galfride. All of this was my fault for not resisting the pull to medieval time.

Lying in bed next to Sophie, I relaxed, knowing both my kids were under my roof, safe for the moment. Otho was contented in the tropics, and Galfride was held captive by Ylva. I felt certain Otho could not penetrate the barriers formed around my home. I was not so sure about the team of Galfride and Thorgisl.

I lay picturing what Ylva might have done with Galfride once she got to her mountain. He certainly deserved to experience captivity, as my son had said.

Next morning started our weekend together, with Rousseau officially moved west.

"Sophie says this room needs a sliding door out to the

garden. Maybe a little patio with plant pots and a table."

Through the large window, I watched my daughter walking in the yard playing her flute.

Rousseau knelt and lined up a handful of books on one of many empty shelves.

"I've got Joaquin and his guys working on the attic. May as well make the garden accessible from this room, while they're at it."

"I won't invade your space forever," he said, looking up at me. "I'm hoping to see you use this as an office someday." He looked up at me, serious.

"I love having you here."

"I just want to get my feet under me for the East Bay. And…this stuff."

"That's fine, sweety." I ruffled his hair which was buzz-cut on the sides, curly on top. "Sophie'll just be here for the weekend. We can go to Ylva after that, for more training—"

"Dragons." Rousseau shone. He placed the last book from his bag on a shelf and stood. "But you're right, it'd be great work at the desk and see out into the garden. This window's too high for that."

"Especially when Sophie gets me to reproduce Marget's yard."

"That'd be terrific."

As I made an omelet and brewed coffee, I told him about the dark place Galfride had created that allowed Thorgisl to break into our scrying, then Ylva's dragon burning it away. I filled him in on Marget sharing Cornish songs and plant lore with Sophie. We brought breakfast outside. Sophie soon emerged.

"Did the sylphs join you?" I asked her.

"Yes, for a bit." She sat and helped herself. "I'm going

to hang out with Ian tonight. He's not playing so we might do English dancing in Caspar."

"He won't perform with them?"

"Not this time. He said he'd dance with me. I want to talk to him about Galfride."

"Great idea. Good to open it up, bring it out in the open."

"That's what I think. The situation needs transparency. Ylva should deal with Ansgor. And the whole Thrizzle thing… It's got to be settled once and for all. I don't want Rousseau ever taken against his will again." She stared at us fiercely.

Rousseau laughed. "Gettin' tough." He flipped her hair.

"Darn right." She turned to me. "Are we sure Otho is happy in Borneo or wherever? Has anyone checked?"

"That might take some scrying. Maybe while you're out with Ian tonight, Rousseau and I can go bug Marget."

"She'd love that," Sophie said. "I've started plotting out the new yard." She pointed at her drawing pad on the other side of the table. "We can look through catalogs for plants. I have my notes from Marget, too."

"We can get more ideas from her, and also Shelley," I said.

"And Bedw," she added.

"First, I think we have to make the soil more fertile. I'm happy to dig up the lawn."

"Like you did in front," Sophie said.

"Yeah. We can make it a haven here. I was thinking of a pond back in the corner."

"That would be excellent." Sophie glowed. "I'm going to do some school work before tonight." She paused. "Unless you had something else in mind. We haven't had much time since I got up here that wasn't involved in—"

"The past? I know, and I feel bad about that. It's—"

"Often fascinating," Rousseau said. "I'm sure Soph would agree with that."

"Yeah." She grabbed a half piece of buttered toast and started for the house. "I'll concede that."

We cleared the breakfast to the kitchen. Entering the living room, Rousseau stopped. "Is this a new weaving?" He approached, studying it. "I think I know what this is."

"Does the color tone give it away?"

"That, and I get a feeling from it. It's Esch isn't it? And what's this in the shadows? Some fae creature."

"Believe it or not, that's the...being we found in Geestendorf. The Trader of the Stone."

"She's healthy now. That's the way she's supposed to be. In her world." His voice conveyed awe. "You did that. You and Ylva. You got them both back where they belong. I feel something, just from the image of the stone. That love-feeling you described. I sense it."

I came to stand by him and put my arm around his waist.

"Wow. This design came to you, and you wove it?"

"I didn't even know what I was weaving 'til I was done," I said.

"That's whack. Have they started on the attic? Let's go see."

We climbed the ladder, ducked under and stepped over construction materials. The smell of sawdust scented the air.

"At least the cobwebs and dust motes are getting scattered," I said.

An opening had been cut for a balcony. Rousseau squatted at the corner of a protective sheet, lifted it and looked out. "This'll be awesome."

"I think so, too."

"If we made a little tower, we could probably see the sea."

The day went quickly. When Sophie left, Rousseau and I walked to Marget's. I sent her a text and then a little mental ping. She responded gaily. "Please do come."

We stopped at the garden and harvested parsnips. I also plucked herbs I knew she favored, and we walked on. Rousseau chatted about starting his legal practice both here and in the East Bay. We discussed our trip to Ylva.

At Marget's back fence, Rousseau asked, "Has Marget made the front yard safer? It seems like Galfride was free to do anything up there with no one the wiser."

"I think his instruments made that possible," I said. "No one knows much about them. Not even Ylva."

"I bet she'll find out now, with him her captive."

"I bet, too." We shared a pained but delighted smile.

"Can you teach me to go through?" Rousseau asked. "On my own?"

"I use enchanted jewelry. I haven't tried it without." I imagined myself on the other side and found I was in the same spot as before. I shrugged. "I'm sure there are techniques, or magicks, without the rings. I just haven't learned them."

He took my hand. "Okay." He grinned. "Later."

We appeared in Marget's yard, walked up the path and climbed her steps. As we did, I let her know we were there.

She opened the door with a happy smile, wiping her hands on her apron. "Welcome. I was just baking."

"I smell it." Rousseau kissed her cheek. "I hope you'll make the sweet berry oggy again sometime." He quickly amended, "But whatever you're baking smells delicious."

"Ha." She swatted him lightly with a wooden spoon. "I barely put it in the oven." Her cheeks had grown rosy in that instant.

My son *was* charming.

"Oh. Maybe it's the oven I smell." He grinned. "Or just the idea."

"Cheeky. I'm glad you liked the oggy. My son loves it so I'll be making it often. Sit. Let's talk over tea." She already had the water steaming and poured for each of us.

Rousseau brought the cup to his nose. "Mm. Mint."

"With a few other things. You had quite a night." She gave him a warm, steady gaze.

He took a tentative sip. "Yeah. Last night was...crappy."

"No better word for it, son." Marget sounded angry.

"I hope this Galfride thing gets put to rest, with Ylva's help," I said. "We're going Monday to *Galdhøpiggen*. Maybe we can have a kind of council. What do you think? Bring Ian?"

"Yes." She nodded emphatically and appeared grateful. "I think that's the only way."

"I was asking Mom about Otho," Rousseau said, "thinking we might try scrying to see if he's staying in the tropics." Rousseau turned his cup slowly on the table.

"I understand," Marget said. "You don't want to be taken by surprise, grabbed again. Yes, let's check. But Ylva will have the best connection for that. She brought them there and has kept watch."

"Oh, I brought parsnips." I rose to wash them and the herbs I'd picked from the gardens.

Marget stood. "Delightful. I can make mash to go with dinner. I'll put them to boil now."

Chapter 13

After dinner and clean up, we climbed the stairs to the attic.

Marget said, "I'm glad we don't have to worry about Galfride for the moment. Since he followed us to this time, I haven't rested easy for a moment."

"Me, either," I said. "I'm also worried about Thorgisl. When Ylva and I talked to him, I thought we'd made progress, but I can't help the sense that he's still planning."

"Because that's who he is. The situation with Esch is not settled."

"He was shocked, though, that the Stone is not amber. I hoped he might lose all interest."

"He'll still be curious about Esch's properties," she said.

Rousseau examined carved objects on the shelves near the altar.

"Most likely. I was in his mind so many times but he only kept me in outer chambers of it. I don't really know how much he obsesses about one thing. He kidnapped Boldo, wanting to get the Stone through his connection to Otho. Even attacked their clan and held Mora hostage all that time."

We grew somber remembering the state she'd been in when finally captured back.

"But he so delighted in the dragon baby. I hoped that might replace his obsession." I settled on a cushion by the scrying bowl.

"Once a greedy mage, always one." Marget sat across from me.

I said, "Ylva asked why he wants the power. He scoffed. Like, 'Why would anyone not always hunger for more?' The scary part is, now I think he's focused on Duff's ability to find power stones."

Rousseau walked over to join us on another pillow.

"I know Ylva didn't like that." Marget uncovered the bowl.

"No, she didn't. And I know she's strong. He mentioned Ice Giants, too. I've heard the myths. I wonder if it's a real thing. I mean, we've seen dragons now."

Rousseau fumed, "It's so wrong that he can put everyone on edge like this."

"It is," I agreed. "Ylva may have a way of putting the fear into him, or monitoring him, at least. I hope so, but at the moment he has Duff and all her people to threaten her with. What does *he* love enough to make him vulnerable, and protective?" I thought, of course, of the way he looked at Frigon.

As Marget lit candles, I constellated my brand and felt unmarred safety all around the house.

We took hands and slowed our breathing. Marget began a chant. We echoed, repeating her Old Cornish words. I sensed the meanings. Vibrant intuitive energies lit up in my body and mind. I felt the same happening in Rousseau and Marget. The surface of the water showed a scene across oceans. We sensed the scrying spell searching islands for Otho and his ship. Briefly, I wished Ylva were with us, but then put my trust in us.

I felt Boldo then, in my mind. "Greetin's, wayfarin' Angel. Ye seem t' be searchin' for m' cousin."

I affirmed. "We are."

He said, "Ye won't find him in southern islands."

I experienced a moment of fear. "Do you know where he is?"

"Aye. Right here. He and his men came with presents from th' tropics. Th' others have left. His ship sits at anchor no' far off. The blighter wants t' stay on land fer a bit, spend time with the clan."

"That's good," I said. "Isn't it?"

"T'is good, aye. He left as a young fella, on bad terms with his people, and with th' law, I wouldn't be surprised. I'll tell ye one day, when we're sittin' by a fire, with a cup o' ale. When's that time gonna come, sweet Ceirwyn?"

He used the Welsh name chosen for me by Baird when he'd passed me off as Kyna's cousin in medieval time. Most still used it.

My heart swelled, longing for the moment he described. I'd popped in, in spirit form, next to their campfires, but never stayed to experience their camp in a restful way. "Soon, I hope. Thank you for catching us and giving this news. I'll tell the others what you've told me."

"Don't make me wait too long, Angel."

I wanted to promise. But life held little predictability these days. "I'll try." As we broke contact, I realized Marget and Rousseau had been watching me. The scrying picture had gone.

"Sorry. That was Boldo. He says Otho is with the Silwy in the north of Wales. Otho's men have left but he's stayed, wanting to make amends with his clan, I think."

"Do you think it's sincere?" Marget asked. "It wouldn't be a trick, would it?"

"I hope it's sincere. That would make it more likely that he's not a threat to Rousseau. Now his mother is back, he has a chance—"

"Mora's Otho's mother?" Rousseau asked, surprised.

"Yes," I said. "Boldo's aunt. They're cousins."

"What made him be...the way he was? Rough brigand or whatever. Do you know?"

"I don't. He angered the clan. Broke a pretty important rule, I'd say. Then he was on the run, maybe didn't feel like he could return. Set himself up as a pirate for hire."

Rousseau said. "I hope he's one less medieval person to worry about."

"But I don't want anyone to be able to grab you, whether it's him or someone else. The more training you get, the better." A lump in my throat ached. "I feel guilty that I've put you in harm's way."

"It might not be you. The same way Kyna had a resonance with you, some of them have been drawn to me. Like Gwynedd calling to me, and Baird coming to me on the underground train. You didn't do that."

"Maybe. Maybe they felt similar vibrations in you to mine, though. I guess we can't be sure. Like Baird, searching for Kyna, found me in this time using the gold crystal I'd been in. What was he following, really? The spirit. Then I deliberately searched, with ancient language and writing, trying to find my way back to Baird's time, and that's how I connected with Kyna."

"Only after they'd found you," he said, remembering the order of events as I'd told them, that the Samhain encounter at the oak tree was five years after the Winter Solstice when I'd been drawn into Kyna's spirit in medieval time, seemingly through writing the Solstice *after*!

"Time is a twisted cord we may never unravel," I said.

"I think we can," my son said, confident.

Marget listened, glancing back and forth between us, her own thoughts clearly percolating. "Shall we go downstairs for dessert and something hot to drink?" She got to her feet, using Rousseau's shoulder and a hand-up. "Thank you, son." To me, she said, "He's a gem, you know." There was a sadness in her voice. I knew she wanted to find Ian again, as a fond and doting son, if it were possible.

"I have a lot more questions," Marget said, grinning at me as we descended the stairs. "For instance, what's the deal with Boldo?"

I might have blushed but said only, "He's always been grateful to me for saving him."

Rousseau and I walked home late, after dessert.

Sophie arrived soon after and joined us in the living room. I'd built a small fire.

"How was it?" I asked.

"Dancing was fun. Then we climbed down to a beach and walked."

"That sounds great. Were you able to discuss Galfride?"

"Yeah, I told him what the butthead did to Rousseau yesterday. He sounded disgusted. I asked him how much he remembers from their childhood friendship. He said Marget, with Ylva's help, brought a lot of it back to him, but his mom didn't know everything about what he and Galfride had got up to. He said he wasn't going to tell me because it seems sick now. And hearing everyone's stories about everything since then, he doesn't have much desire to renew the friendship."

"But Galfride can be very persuasive," I said, wanting hope to seep in from what she was telling us, but hardly daring to. "He could even put a spell on him until he's convinced him."

"I don't think it could last. But that's why we have to make sure he gets more training, too. Mom," she put her hand on my arm, "he said he sees why his mom brought him here, even why she had to suppress his memories, so that the connection with Galfride would be broken, even though it made his life really hard for a long time. He was furious when he first got his memories back." She teared up.

"He lost all those years with her. That's got to hurt. But she never would have made him forget her as well. Not on purpose. She should have had more help, instead of just threats, from the Cornish Council of Witches."

"Yeah, but now he says he gets it. He even has said he's glad he's mostly been in this time, after seeing the rough life they lived a thousand years ago."

"Really? That's good. I hope he tells his mom that."

"I think he will. Or she'll just know, soon enough. It's so fun to go to her house. It's like she's the perfect combination—magic from the past, and also talented in modern ways."

"You wish I had a bigger house," I said, then groaned, hearing my defensiveness.

"Mom, you keep saying that. I like your cottage. You get more smell of the sea here, too."

"Do you think so?"

"Sometimes I hear it. The rumble of the shoreline. It's like an ebb and flow."

"Besides, this is what we inherited from Gramma and Grampa," said my pragmatic son.

"True enough. Well, I'm off to bed." I stood.

"I'm heading back to Berkeley in the morning," said Sophie, "not super early but, you know, after breakfast. I guess you're not coming to the East Bay yet, Rouss?"

"No. I'm going to help get things sorted out here first. What's happening with you and Ian?"

"He's getting a lift with me," she said.

"That's good. You two are getting along," I said.

"We are. Tonight felt like the most direct conversation we ever had."

I felt a mix of trepidation and relief that she was keeping him close. It seemed like a time when he'd need stability, from more than just his mom. He still had residual anger, naturally, and would need someone else to talk to.

When Ian arrived in the morning, he told Sophie he would stay the day and see her in the East Bay that night.

He drove off, turning left at the end of the block, east, toward his mother's house.

Sophie prepared to leave on her own. "That's cool. I can listen to audio books on the drive." She grinned, bouncing back easily, in her usual ebullient way.

Joaquin and a couple of other men pulled into the space Ian had vacated.

Rousseau hugged Sophie, then followed the work crew as they circled around the side of the house.

Since Sophie had shortened her visit, it looked like we could move up the time table on our trip to train with Ylva.

Ylva had pressed for training to happen sooner and she'd been right—Galfride had snatched Rousseau around the time she'd been emphasizing the urgency.

By afternoon, Rousseau and I were at Marget's, ready to travel to Norway of a thousand years ago. Rousseau wore the heavy wool sweater Ylva had given him. Marget had brought a thick pullover for Ian, and a long wool coat for herself. We locked arms. I sent a mental message to Ylva, who brought us to behind her home, a little way up the hill. Ian and Rousseau started walking toward her house, we three women following.

The day was spent in alpine air, Duff showing Ian and Rousseau his workshop, Marget and I learning about Ylva's cold larder under the house for the winter months, and her garden area, warmed from below by fires in a deep oven.

Rousseau gave Ian a tour around the rest of the house. He detected my presence in his mind and responded that it was fine if I listened in; he'd tell me if that changed.

In the top room where Ylva kept an altar, he described to Ian how Baird and Boldo had played music in there during Mora's healing.

"I'd like to hear them play the old instruments," Ian said. "Who's Thorgisl?"

"He's been the biggest pain, other than Galfride," Rousseau explained bluntly. "Though I guess Ansgor was pretty bad for a while."

"So where dwells this biggest pain?" Ian asked, fingering Ylva's smooth stone carvings of animals that appeared on surfaces throughout the house.

"In a Jutland fort." He glanced at Ian, then added, "A point of land jutting up from North Germany and Denmark. My mom first encountered him when she saved a Traveler from the fort's dungeons. He can put fevers on people that can't be cured, stick amber under their skin to track them. Quite an unsavory fellow."

"You've met him?"

"Yeah. Couple times. He held me hostage. But I offered to do it, to save the leader of the Silwy."

"This is all bizarre, isn't it?"

Rousseau laughed. "Yeah. It is. An adventure, when it's not horrifying."

"You'll have to tell me more about the horrifying as well as the adventure."

We called them for dinner.

After, Ylva walked with us by torchlight to the caves where Esch had been kept. The back door opened.

I hurried to talk to her. "Are you sure you want him to know about the cave? Maybe the ceremonial ground would be better."

Chapter 14

I an? Or Galfride?" Ylva asked. "I can contain them best in the caves. I have Galfride in a similar stasis to the one he put on your son, and on Gwynedd from what I've been told."

"That's fair," I said, sending her a picture of Gwynedd, held that way for months.

She looked at me, jaw set in a hard line.

At the dark entrance, a second torch burst into flame as Ylva took it from its wall notch. After weaving through tunnels, the six of us, including Duff, came to the small cavern where we'd communicated with Esch so intensely. *Galdhøpiggen* still held the residue of mountain-love I'd felt in such a powerful burst then. I thought Ylva might have purposely put Galfride where he could feel it, too.

The man, bundled in warm clothes, sat on cushions against a wall, a blanket over him. A heater globe hovered near. These were kindnesses he had not afforded his captives.

We sat in a circle around him, on stuffed hides.

Ylva brought Galfride to consciousness, saying, "You will not be able to disappear," in a less than friendly tone. "Ian and Rousseau are here, as well as Kay. I believe you might have something to say to them."

Galfride studied the two young men with angry faces,

then turned his gaze to me. "Kyna's cousin," he drawled. "You are always in the middle of so much meddling. All of you." He scanned the rest. "I only attempted to renew what was an…affectionate boyhood friendship."

"Is that what it was?" Ylva asked. "Or were you using him, as you use everyone."

"You tire me, witch. You provoke me. You are not even of our people."

"And what people would that be? Germanic? Welsh? Wanderer? You were trained by the Wanderers, saved by them, given shelter and food by them, and how do you repay them?"

"I trained myself, witch."

"Oh really? I believe you learned from Marget's books, as well. Were you not allowed into the Druid school based on Wanderers' training and vouching?"

I'd wondered how he did, in fact, get into the Druid school.

"You mistake me for Baird and Kyna. I came from a powerful lineage in Saxony. We have natural gifts, as does my niece, Branwyn."

"I see. And no one has ever helped you learn?"

Galfride got a far-away look, seeming to remember something. Ylva spirit-jumped, following the trail in his mind, helping him retrieve whatever memories he sought.

She shared the picture with all of us: a boy sitting with other children, learning from a woman who appeared kind.

"I did learn as a child. I'd forgotten Gret." His expression softened. Then grew hard again. "Ansgor brought back some of my memories, with a box of objects. I don't know how he got them from my youth. But…I feel more of it…"

His face contorted, consternation blended with emotions as Ylva tapped memories, of family, childhood friends, innocence. Tears wet his cheeks, unbidden.

"How could I have forgotten so much?" He leaned forward, pressing his hands to his face.

"Your family had a particular relationship with Ansgor. Is that right?" Ylva asked, detecting a clue.

He shrugged. "I was only a child."

"You have memories in your deeper mind, of things you heard and saw. Gifts came to your parents. What did they do for him? Spy on the neighboring town?"

Scraps of remembered conversation and incidents trickled into his mind. Ylva shared them.

Ian and Rousseau sat silent, fascinated. Galfride's focus seemed to be held by Ylva. She had remained standing, gripping an elaborately carved staff.

"You were the eldest," she pressed on. "You didn't approve. You argued with them about it. When they torched Kyna and Duff's village, you left, forever. Were you banished? Ashamed? Angry?"

"I...heard the Wanderers call to Kyna. I'd...admired her. When Duff carried her to the wagons, I followed." His hands worked, now pressed into his lap. "I hid in the back of a wagon, under covers. They found me. But they were kind."

"As was Marget, was she not?" Ylva asked.

"Okay, sure, fine. I was an angry youth. You want an apology? I apologize." He gave a mocking bow from his seated position.

"We all want for you to come to a new place in your mind, to never feel the need to kidnap, hold anyone hostage, harm others' minds," she said.

"What if I don't come to that 'place in my mind'?" he sneered. "What're you gonna do, witch. Keep holding me hostage in this shithole cave?" He glanced toward Ian at last.

Both young men had been in Ylva's mind, seeing and

hearing everything. Both had received Ylva's healing presence before this. I did not think they were feeling very sympathetic.

"I want you and Ian to talk now," Ylva said. "This is a council, Galfride. Make no mistake. I could have made it far harsher, with my full clan. You deserve punishment for your crimes against others. Yet, I see you had difficult beginnings, and suffered. It seems that, for whatever reason, no one has tried to work with you. Perhaps you made that impossible, hiding in your caves in les Haute Alpes, and your lavish life in castles."

Galfride's expression said he'd disappear to those caves or castles this instant if given half a chance.

Ian spoke. "Galfride. I do remember some good times in our friendship. I also recall what we did to others." His gaze dropped to his hands and he grimaced. "I don't feel great about that. Granted, we were young. But I don't see an alliance between us. I don't know much about your purpose. Maybe if you told me, it could make a difference. But...my life is music now. I have a good time. I remember the past, and I feel pretty whole." He laughed, a self-deprecating sound, then checked Galfride's face. "I think, over time, if you still want, I might like to visit Cornwall with you, remember old times. But things you're doing? Like holding Rousseau frozen? That was just plain shitty." He glanced around. "Sorry."

Galfride stretched out a leg, moved his shoulders, and looked around at all of us, then looked back at Ian. "You make me feel churlish. Yeah, I had a lot of anger. And was searching...for something. I knew something about power. I guess I got lost along the way. I blocked out memories of the past. Not sure how it happened. Maybe just being far from my people, they slipped away. When Ansgor showed me my things, it seemed the answer. I remembered Kyna's past, too, in Germania. I needed to find her. I wanted—" He stopped abruptly.

"You played with your niece's mind before that, Galfride," said Ylva. "You performed reprehensible tasks for powerful men, so that you could live richly. Come on. Be honest. It didn't start with Ansgor."

Galfride shrugged. "Fine. What if I promise to be good. Will you let me go?"

"Your confinement has been far shorter than what you submitted Branwyn and Gwynedd to."

"I think hot branding irons might be better than this endless nattering. At least it'd be over with."

Ylva said, "That can be arranged as well. But there'll be more nattering. Make no mistake."

"Okay. I don't want that. Thank you for being so kind and only talking my ears off."

Gods, he was so incurably rude. I shook my head.

He looked at me. "Do you delight in this, Kay?" He said my name with that sarcastic twist, referencing my first deceptions with him. Gods, he did not forgive what he perceived as *others'* slights.

"You were the one wanting to tell me of your past, in your caves," I said. "I did not ask for a situation in which I had to dissemble."

"I thought ye were Kyna," he growled.

"No, you didn't," I said.

My son stared back and forth from me to Galfride.

"Alright. I wanted ye to help me get t' my son."

"Hamelyn. Right. Was he going to be your replacement for Ian?"

Ian gasped.

Galfride stared at him. "Nay. 'Course not. I wanted t'…"

He searched for words. "I wanted to help th' lad, so he wouldn't be alone like I'd been. I mean—" he held up a hand to me as I started to protest— "alone in his abilities."

"He's a marvelous young man. A great craftsman and musician," I said. "He composes music and collects histories. He has a loving family. A *father* who's been there for him. He's learning his abilities, too. Healthy magic, to the level of standing with The Thirteen. How is that 'alone with his abilities'?"

"He has other abilities," Galfride shouted and tried to lurch toward me but was stopped by the shield Ylva kept around him.

"Oh, yes, like snatching the memories of a thirteen-year-old girl to see what happens? Making her force someone to kill himself?" I didn't know how I knew that. Maybe it was Kyna's memory.

"You did that again?" Ian asked, alarmed.

Marget held her stomach, looking green.

"Oh, come on. Ye exaggerate." But Galfride's voice had less force.

"No, she doesn't," Ylva said, "but I think we've uncovered enough for today. Everyone's feeling a might ill, I believe."

Galfride dropped back against the wall, face twisted in a snarl.

I didn't want to leave it that way. I constellated my brand, touching the rings and silver together, activating the sense of love that had built in me and Ylva in this mountain cavern, with Esch. I made up, in my mind, a kind of chant. "Let love prevail. May this man be healed, along with Ian."

Ylva picked up the mantra, and then Marget, and Rousseau. I noticed when Ian's mind join ours. The feeling swelled to euphoria.

Galfride would have fought it but it was too good. His face sagged, lost its sardonic posturing. He stared up at us, surprised, then laughed, a tough, reflex bark.

I could only hope the feeling would stay with him.

"Do you think I can release you now?" Ylva asked him.

"Am I cured of evil, ye mean?" he asked, but his voice did not carry the taint of eternal anger. He stood, tested the range of his confinement. He was able to stand to his full 5'11"—a considerable height for that time, especially in Wales.

We all stood. He came forward, tentative, but no shield held him. I thought Ylva could probably snap him out of the air if he did try leaving too soon.

He took Ian's hand. "I hope we can spend time, at some future juncture," he said.

Ian shook his hand back, nodding hesitantly.

Galfride turned to Rousseau. "I do apologize," he said, sounding slightly whiny.

Well, how much could we expect. He'd been surly so long.

"I like you. I wouldn't—" He glanced around. It was clearly excruciating to be so sincere. "—wouldn't want to ruin what—" He shrugged.

Rousseau, ever the peace-maker, gave him a hug. "It's okay, man. We're good."

I had to smile, almost letting out a giddy bark of my own.

Galfride grinned then, threw back his head and laughed a real laugh. "We're good. We're good." He turned away, as if to leave.

"You'll have further apologies to make, eventually," Ylva said. "How about a couple more, just to round things out."

Galfride turned back. To Marget, he said, "I'm sorry I treated your hospitality badly." Before she could form a response, he turned to me. "I suppose you want one, too."

"How about when they can be sincere," I said, and turned to leave the cave before the others. How he could trigger me.

Chapter 15

B ehind me, I heard him say, "Ceirwyn. Kyna's faux-cousin. I apologize for snatching you from Kyna's home where you were playing wife with Baird. I apologize for grabbing you from the cave under Aberffraw, where you were doing the same, even impersonating her at a dinner party. It was too easy. Weren't they trainin' ye at all?"

"That's enough," Ylva said.

I turned and made myself say, "I thank you for coming to my aid when Duff was ill. You've helped us several times and I'm grateful. Though I'm still not entirely sure why you did."

He looked puzzled. "Didn't ye know? Kyna asked me. She'd never asked me for anythin' before."

"And what was it when you helped get my son back from Otho's ship?"

"Well, I like the kid." He winked at Rousseau.

"And now? The Stone? Thorgisl? Ian? Ansgor? What's your stance? What are you going to do with yourself, with your life?" Ylva asked.

He turned to her. "Are ye going to try to buy my cooperation by givin' me a dragon like Thorgisl's?"

"I don't *give* dragons," Ylva said. "And don't think for

a moment that he couldn't leave, or that his safety is not guarded at all times. He cannot be used for ill-purpose."

"Is that true? That tight a rein, eh?"

But I sensed that Galfride was hoping for one.

"Alright, well, I'll be off." He bowed to each of us in turn.

Ian looked as if he might step toward him but stayed back.

When Galfride had walked a few steps, he disappeared.

Ylva said, "I think I'll make it difficult for him to go to your time for a while. I still have some work to do with him. But, Kay, your chant with the mountain was genius."

I beamed, proud. "It felt good to me."

Everyone agreed it was a great feeling.

"Let's return home, shall we?" Marget said, grasping Ian's arm and mine. "We don't need to occupy more of Ylva's time."

"What about the training?" Rousseau asked.

"How tired are you?" Ylva looked at Rousseau, then Ian.

The young men exchanged glances.

"I can go on a while," Ian said.

Rousseau nodded agreement.

We walked to the house. I felt like dropping on the nearest couch. It had been an intense encounter.

We snacked. Then, bundled again in warm clothes, we passed down a sleeping street. An owl hooted. A hawk screeched overhead. Those were the only sounds besides the crunching of our boots. At the ceremonial ground, I was surprised to see numerous tall figures clustered around a bonfire. Ylva introduced us to her clansmen and -women who became a sea of large hands, white teeth catching firelight as they spoke greetings.

I wondered what would be different about this training, that it needed so many. Or did they just all want to be part of it? To impress, the fanfare of her kin might be a good touch.

Ylva brought Rousseau and Ian long robes. Metal and bone shapes attached to them clanked and clacked when the young men moved.

The ceremony began with drumming and chanting. I saw it was going to be more than a lesson in mental protection. They learned to enter the minds of birds and soar with them. I joined Rousseau's mind, to see what he saw.

Was this to seduce especially Ian into wanting to learn more? I didn't see how it would help them protect themselves.

The highlight came when a dragon landed up the hill. At last, Ylva gave intense lessons in mind-reading and mind-protection, with the dragon help.

In the end, the young men—Marget's son and mine—were rewarded with a dragon ride. I didn't think Ylva could have pulled off a much more convincing or life-changing extravaganza.

When we at last made our way back up the road, walking between peaked, Scandinavian-style homes of a thousand years ago, I was dead-tired and thinking of my own bed. But Ylva said, "Why don't you stay the night. I've tested the amber pieces—the one taken from Boldo's hand and the one given to Rousseau. I believe Duff can shape rings for the boys that protect and give powers. We'll need to experiment to develop the right powers."

We found out there were more sleeping spaces on the second level of Ylva's home, and beds enough for all.

Next day, Duff measured for rings and got to work. Once shaped and fitted, Ylva spent time enchanting them, as Aelfwyn had done with my medieval bling.

"What about a tattoo like yours, Mom? Isn't that what you use to make spaces safe from eavesdropping?"

"My brand? I don't know what-all went into it. Aelfwyn and Duff put magic into the brand itself, and Aelfwyn had, I think, special salves."

"Ylva, do you use branding in that way? Or tattooing? Do they increase your powers?" Rousseau asked.

We'd seen intricate tattoos on the backs of hands and on necks, even faces, in firelight the night before.

"My kin earn markings for deeds they've performed, or new discoveries they've made, that sort of thing," Ylva explained.

"Do they impart magical abilities?"

"They give them honor." Ylva laughed. "The branding of The Thirteen is something I have not fully explored, but I have been intrigued."

"You helped heal mine," I said to her.

"I want to feel what it's like when you constellate it. Isn't that what you call it?"

"Yes," I said. "Would you like to now?"

"Indeed."

"Do you want to join us, in my mind?" I asked Rousseau.

Not to leave Ian out, I said, "You're welcome, as well," though the thought of the surly young man entering my mind did not sit entirely well with me.

He looked tempted to shrug, but after all he'd experienced lately, it wasn't in him.

Figuring Marget would come along, I opened, then traced the sigils on my back until the heron shape lit up. I centered the energy in my heart and sent it outward. It surrounded the house, and I sensed, with clarity, whether it was clear of negative minds or powers. I felt the others with me. This was a first, similar to being in the Circle but different from those trained minds.

I let it recede back to normal and released their minds from mine.

Ylva spoke first. "That's marvelous. I've never done anything quite like it."

This revelation from the superlative magic-worker amazed me.

"Awesome." Rousseau put his hands on my shoulders and shook me lightly. "I want to be able to do that."

"Maybe you can, just with your ring. I never thought to do exactly that when I had only my rings and the pendant. The branded sigil sort of taught me." I gave a sheepish chuckle, not sure how that would sound to others.

"Sometimes the tools teach us," Ylva agreed.

Ian wore a look I'd never seen. I thought back to his envious glares toward my gold crystal. This expression held new self-assurance and joy. He seemed more "whole" than ever.

Looking intense, Rousseau said to Ylva, "I'm searching for that feeling but I only get it when in your mind."

"These things take time," Ylva said. "Practice each day. I'll look into the brands and tattoos. First, the rings."

"How'm I gonna practice? Go creeping into other people's minds? Just kidding."

"With good intention. There are all different levels. There are polite ways, and intimate ones. You'll find what's needed. You can join into animals' minds as well. Especially practice testing for invasive thoughts as they first enter, or try to. Get your mom to test you. Practice the ice wall for protecting parts of your mind."

"Did you ever get a chance to check on Ansgor?" I asked her.

"Yes. He's growing old and frail. He's moved down into the village and is cared for there. That's probably what Galfride discovered."

As we prepared to leave, I thought how strange it would be not to wonder if Ansgor was plotting against someone we cared about. "So, he's really no threat. That's your belief?"

"None."

Well, I could strike one alliance with Galfride off my list of worries.

At Marget's, we helped prepare lunch, and ate in mystified silence. So much had happened. Had Galfride really changed at all?

"The only real threat now seems to be Thorgisl," Marget said. "Sorry. I hope I didn't ruin your meal."

"Oh, no, he's never far from my thoughts. I don't want it to remain that way. I want these guys to enjoy their powers, not to need them for defense against dangerous high-jackings and so on."

"I want that, too." She looked at her son. "How are you feeling about it all?"

Ian chewed for a moment. When he'd swallowed, he said, "Now I know some of the possibilities, and the great feelings that can come from…good magic." He quirked a half-grin at me, and I thought he was remembering the love-chant in the caves. "I just want to live my regular life for a while—play music, spend time with this guy's sister." He turned his charismatic, cross-tooth smile on Rousseau. "And give it all a chance to settle. Then I'd like to go back, see our old house in Cornwall," he said to his mom. He shrugged.

"And Galfride?" she asked.

"I meant what I said in the caves. I don't feel great about what we did. I don't *understand* what we did. I've been crappy to girls sometimes, during…the Time of Forgetting, I guess I'll call it."

Marget frowned. When he saw this, he hurried on, "Nothing like that. Just kind of a prick sometimes. But I don't want to be shitty. There was a feeling, in the cave. You know, it reminded me of those dreams where you feel someone knows you completely? That kind of close feeling you never have in waking life?"

We all nodded.

"That's what it felt like. And…I know I'm getting kind of sappy, but I feel like part of it stuck in me. Like it painted me new. Maybe I'm still just in the thrall of it, but—"

"I know what you mean," Rousseau said. "I still feel it, too."

Marget and I both agreed that we'd had similar experiences. I didn't want to say that was Esch. I didn't want to build any idea that if he had the Stone of Arkoss, he'd always feel that way. I thought it was a combination of the mountain and elements, a spell I'd built between it all.

"Well, I think we should head home," I said, getting up and taking dishes to the sink.

"I have to go, too." Ian hugged his mom, kissed her

cheek. "I'm driving down to Berkeley tonight."

"Alright. I hope to see you soon."

"You will."

By his car, we all parted, waving to Marget.

"Want a lift?" he asked us.

I glanced at Rousseau, thinking he might be tired.

"Thanks, I think I'd like to walk. You?" he asked me.

I agreed and we set off after waving.

"So, what are you going to do about Thorgisl?" Rousseau asked.

"I'll keep talking to Ylva and Marget until we have a plan."

"Do you really think Galfride's not a danger anymore?" he asked as we rounded the first corner.

"I'm not sure at all," I answered, honestly.

Chapter 16

As we passed through neighborhoods of one-story, fifties-style houses, I said, "I wonder if we made any difference at all. I can't believe regaining more early memories won't change him. But I'm curious what he'll be like after this. He's so inscrutable. And such positive feelings can be fleeting."

"I wish I could have stayed knowing him the way he was at first."

"Better to know the truth, though, don't you think?"

"I suppose. Yeah. I just meant he hadn't been mean to me, and he'd been helping you guys. I hoped he'd changed already. I never imagined him doing that to me." He was quiet for half a block, then asked, "Do you think, if no one drew you to the past, you'd still go? I mean, now. From now on. If you don't learn of any danger?"

"It's weird. I've formed relationships. It's like another neighborhood." I waved my arm around us at the houses, silent and dark. "I can't imagine abandoning that. I've seen Marget's home in Ancient Cornwall. I can't say I'll never choose to return there, or to Kyna's home." I took his hand.

"But...that worries me. You've continually found situations that threw you into danger."

I squeezed his hand. "Could you say you wouldn't go back?" I caught his thought of the dragon ride.

"No. I understand. But I worry. And I don't want to worry forever."

"I get that. I don't want to worry about you, either. Do you think it might be a matter of training? Of getting stronger?"

He pulled his hand from mine and threw his arm around my shoulders. "Yeah. That's right. That's what we'll do."

In the evening, we toasted marshmallows at the fireplace and watched a favorite old movie. When it ended, we checked email.

"A college friend is wondering if I'm still going to take his room in Oakland," Rousseau said.

"It can be hard to find a place there. Will you take it?"

"I'm thinking about it. In fact, I'm pretty sure I will."

The next day, he rented a van and loaded it with the boxes from storage. By early afternoon, he was on the road to the East Bay and his new home.

Did that mean he trusted that all was safe, all was solved?

Once again, with a quiet home to myself, I wandered around, tucking things away, tidying up, getting back to normal.

But it wasn't normal. Both my kids were on the West Coast now, in easy driving distance. I stopped midway, book in-hand to put away on a shelf in the guest room, gripping the amber ring that was supposed to connect me with Baird. Was there a word, a magical action, that created that tie, like the boots put me in touch with Boldo? Turn it three times or something? I set the book in its place and was about to experiment with the new ring when a knock came at the door.

Chapter 17

Possibilities ran through my mind. Marget? Shelley? Joaquin needing to do something on the construction?

As I reached for the doorknob, I suddenly knew who it was, and dread filled me.

I opened anyway. There stood Galfride.

He studied me, as if *I'd* been the one to pop up on *his* doorstep. "Aren't you goin' to invite me in?"

"I'm not sure," I said. "Should I?"

"I'm not here t' harm ye. Or yer son."

"Well, that's dandy of you. What are you here for, then?" I didn't open the door any wider, kept it four inches open, ready to slam it shut.

I was safe when he was outside—the sylphs had seen to that—but not if he came in.

He shifted, seeming out of his comfort zone for once. "I don't exactly know. It seemed to me that I needed to be here."

"Here? In my house?" I asked, unclear and suspicious.

"As in, with you." His lips curled, but more in self-effacing than his usual sardonic sneer-smile.

"With…me? I don't understand." I glanced behind me, back at him. "Rousseau isn't here." I couldn't take in his words, mind blocked by confused suspicion.

"I can't shake the feelin'. Can I please enter? I want to talk t' you."

What had his talk led to in the past? Mind-control. Unbidden intimacy in order to achieve an unsavory end. "I don't trust you," I blurted out.

Ylva came into my mind then. "I'm monitoring him. If you wish to find out what's on his mind, you will be safe. I will come there if you need me."

Heaving a sigh that blended relief, frustration and self-consciousness, I shot her a mental thank you and pulled the door open further. He stepped through, his fine cape scraping the doorway, and gave me a bow, then strode down the hall as if he owned the place.

I scanned my mind for what he might encounter in the living room. I'd covered the Esch tapestry. What else would he see?

"Can I get you any refreshment?" I asked, hurrying to follow him.

The living room felt small with just him and me. Should we go into the backyard? But that was the special place Sophie and I were cultivating, where the sylphs visited.

"I've added an upstairs. You can see the ocean from up there. I could bring something up. Tea? Biscuits?"

Having carefully studied the living room, taking in the weaving set-up—loom, yarn-filled shelves, spinner—he turned and examined my face, semi-amused with his curled smile. "Certainly. Show the way."

Why was I taking him upstairs? That's where I'd recently added my scrying area.

But I had to get him out of the main house. It seemed imperative. I led the way out to the side stairs and up. At the top, I turned the ornamental handle in the new door with its bevelled-glass insets, feeling proud.

We passed through what was evolving into Marget's magical attic room in miniature, also serving as guest room. My apothecary was hidden in a large ornate armoire I'd scored at a yard sale. Joaquin was building my altar at his house so it wasn't here yet. I kept the scrying bowl inside the armoire to keep it special, and undusty.

But still, not wanting his taint in there, I led swiftly through to the balcony that faced the sea. Finally, I had a view of the ocean that had always been close but invisible to me.

"You could sit here." I pointed to wicker chairs with cushions flanking a round table.

He stepped to the ornate iron balustrade and gazed out.

"I'll just get...those goodies," I said to his back and started away.

His voice followed me. "I don't want to put you t' any trouble."

"No trouble." I rushed away, calling to Ylva in my mind as I trotted down the stairs.

She responded, "I'm here."

"Are you going to listen to...everything?" I asked as I put water on to boil.

She chuckled. "No, dear, just monitoring his thoughts and actions." I felt her smile. "Unless you call for help, or are unconscious."

I grinned, wondering why I'd asked. "That sounds...perfect." In the kitchen, I pulled an unopened package of butter cookies from the cupboard, probably purchased for one of the kids' visits, and placed a number on a plate. Then I switched it for a nicer, one-of-a-kind pottery creation purchased at the local art center. Why was

I trying to impress him? Because he wore nice clothes? Clearly appreciated fine things? That's why he worked for royalty, after all. And lined his pockets for doing nasty things, I reminded myself.

I boiled water and poured it over tea in a small round pumpkin-color pot—the only one I owned with a built-in strainer—expecting a snarky comment from Galfride who'd collected fine items from throughout Europe in his lair in the French Alps. I put it on a tray with cookie plate, lumps of natural sugar and a tiny pitcher of milk.

This was my first time carrying a tray to the attic rooms, and I stepped carefully, setting it on the top step to open the door.

On the balcony, he still stared out.

I set the tray on the small table and sat next to it. Galfride turned and took the other chair. He crossed his legs and gazed at me, serious, brow creased as if...annoyed? What had I done now?

It was odd to see him in my home. In my mind, I skimmed over past encounters. His initial visit to this time had been very recent, but he'd wreaked havoc on our lives in that short span.

He shifted, then recrossed his legs the other way. "Shall I pour out?"

"You can see how strong it's gotten. I'm not that used to black tea."

"Black tea," he mused as he lifted the lid and sniffed. "Well, let's just see." He replaced the lid and poured.

It was as dark as I could stand it. I dolloped milk in mine and watched his face as he poured his.

He plunked a lump of sugar using the tiny pinchers I'd placed on it, and added milk, then lifted and drank. What kind had it been? English Breakfast, I thought.

Something someone else had supplied, in a neat cannister. Maybe my parents. I waited for his reaction.

He stared out at clouds, billowed in the distance, took another gulp and glanced over at me. He seemed to notice something in my expression, for he assured me, "It's very nice."

Who was this polite man, concerned about feelings?

I laughed. "Sorry, I just don't serve—"

"... *black* tea often?" He offered. "What do you usually serve? Tisanes?"

"Mostly. I know for you the default is black tea, so you just call it tea."

"True." He drank more.

I continued making banal conversation. "Some people prefer green. Would you have preferred honey?"

He shook his head, set down his cup and shifted toward me. Impatient with all the niceties, I thought, and heard a light chuckle from Ylva. So, she *was* listening. That was okay, I assured myself. So far.

"That feeling you gave us all," he began. "How did you produce it?"

I pondered, pretty sure I knew what he meant. Then he gave me a mental picture of Ylva's cave. How much did I want to explain? What might I say that wouldn't interest him more in Esch?

"I think what we all felt came from a combination of the mountain itself, the stone, and…maybe a little bit me. Well, my relationship with the others." I breathed hard, heart racing as I recalled the indescribable sensation. Esch responded to my recalling it, from the weaving downstairs, or from the other dimension. I hid the thought behind the ice wall as I set down my cup and sat up straighter. I was sure Ylva was helping to protect Esch. "It was a beautiful feeling," I said at last. "That's why I don't want someone like Thorgisl using the Stone for his ends." I suppose my face and voice might have conveyed pleading by this time.

Galfride picked up a cookie with a chess piece imprinted on the top and appeared to study it. At last, he said, "I understand that. The Stone must be protected."

I leaned forward, surprised. Could he really be an ally? "Someone else in that dimension needs protection. 'Nyad,' someone called her. I'm not sure how any of us can help. That world's air doesn't sustain humans." Was I saying too much?

"I saw that. Your son was choking."

I nodded. "An unpleasant priesthood seems to be in charge. They were ready to put Otho and his crew on trial."

"This intrigues me. Do you not have inventions in your modern era that would sustain life in such a place? Do we need to consult with a...what do you call your alchemists? Scientist? Perhaps we can bring back an air sample somehow."

I realized I'd been thinking only in terms of that time, not of utilizing the tech available now. Who knew what time that world even existed in? I assumed Shagfen needed our help a thousand years ago. But hope had sprung up in me, having someone to share ideas with. It immediately crashed and burned. "You're just trying to get to the Stone." I had started to drink more tea but set it and my half a cookie down, losing appetite.

"No." Galfride stood abruptly. He paced the length of the porch, then stood in front of me. He grabbed my hands and pulled me to standing. His voice lower, he said, "I was beastly t' yeh in th' caves. I'm aware o' that. I'm not...I'm not perfect but I...have changed."

"You do seem different, but—" I tugged at my hands

to pull free, ready to list recent proof he wasn't altogether trustworthy, detecting Ylva on the alert.

He stopped me from speaking with a finger to my lips. "I admit I'm flawed. But for a while now, I've been more interested in your endeavors than my own. My god, you do get yourself mixed up in *baw llanast.*"

Did he really say poopy messes? "Me? What about you? Kidnapping my son in order to get Ian's friendship back? I don't know what else."

"Can I just…may I embrace you?" he asked.

I stared at him, flummoxed.

He pulled me close and laid his cheek against mine, then sniffed my hair. I thought about the plat I'd made in it that morning. Kyna's knowledge told me the pattern meant, "Take heed". I pushed at his chest but he just held me lightly. Finally, I slipped my arms around his slim waist. He smelled of wood fires and earthy stone walls.

He tapped gently on my mind, asking to share things hard to say. Red flags already stood high in my mind. Yet I wanted to hear his thoughts. Ylva sent warnings, that he might try to manipulate me. The subtle could numb you before jabbing, and he was subtle.

Instead of giving me thoughts, he moved his mouth onto mine. I was only partially taken by surprise, and responded.

He broke away first. "I'm sorry. That wasn't what I meant to do." He seemed genuinely confused. Or he was a good actor.

Several comebacks jumped into my head but I found myself saying, "And lonely?" What? Who was controlling my mouth?

He scratched the back of his neck, grinning. "Well, yeh, now that ye mention it."

I backed a step away, to the doorway, and leaned, my back to the jamb. "We have a strange history, you and I. A checkered one."

"Checkered. I don't recognize that term."

"It means like a game board. A mix of good and bad, lately."

"Ah. I see. Or Scottish cloth."

"Indeed." Were we going to finish off with inanities? But safer. Though I'd like to know his true intentions for the Stone, it was a relief. "I have a chess board downstairs I could show you." Now I wanted to get us out of that small cozy area, with its guest bed a few feet away. In fact, I wanted him out of the house. Even out of this time? Heart still racing, I still could not trust the man and his mage powers.

He slouched now against the opposite doorjamb, watching me.

I started for the outer door.

"Shall I help clean up?" He stepped out on the balcony, reaching for the tray.

"It's okay. Leave it."

But he brought the tray with our cups and followed me as I trotted down the outside staircase and entered the living room through the new side door. He set the tray neatly on the built-in breakfast nook table in the kitchen, knocking its surface with his knuckles. "Interesting."

"It's called formica. I'm not sure how it's made, actually. A resin of sorts, I imagine."

He nodded, glancing around the room, at appliances.

"I'll show you the chess board." Unsure why I was pursuing this, I went to the closet in the guest room that was supposed to become my office, and brought out a wood chest. Inside, jade chess pieces snuggled into velvet.

I set them aside, revealing an old chess board made of dark and tan polished squares of wood fitted neatly together.

He plucked a knight from its nest. "I saw a similar game in India."

"My grandparents brought this set from China. The game started in the east. I didn't know it existed a thousand years ago."

"I believe it did. I should go. I wouldn't want to keep you from other—" he glanced around the room— "obligations."

There wasn't a lot to see. Unpacked boxes of books. A fold-out bed. "Did you—" What did I mean to ask. "—accomplish what you wanted? Find out something?" Had he grabbed something from my mind with me unawares? "Where are you off to?" I decided to ask instead. Maybe I shouldn't.

He quirked a brow. "Not sure. Would yeh like to come along?"

I shook my head. "That's okay. I'll get to work on something."

"I'll be off, then." He ambled down the front hall, then turned, hand resting on the knob. "May I return? I do want t' discuss the safety o' the Stone. If you like, I'll prove to you that I'm sincere."

"How would you do that?" I asked, curious.

His face twisted in distaste. "Submit myself to your formidable Norwegi...chieftess," he said with only slight rancor. There was something else on his face. Respect?

"Um. Okay," I said, unsure what else the moment merited.

He left.

Chapter 18

As I closed the door behind him, Boldo's voice came into my head. "That was mighty strange, wouldn't ya say?"

"Good grief. Who all was in my mind for that entire exchange?" I flushed as I stomped down the hall, back into the living room.

"Sorry. I couldn't help sensin' his presence there." Boldo apologized dutifully but perhaps not sincerely. "I owe ye' to keep ye' safe."

"No, I apologize. I don't mean to be grumpy. I appreciate everyone keeping guard."

"I didn't note that kiss a'tall." He suppressed a snicker.

"That does it. I'm not wearing these boots anymore." I plopped into a comfy chair in the living room and started to tug one off.

"Stop! I'm sorry. I didn't mean to see it."

I sat back, so happy to hear my friend's voice, I let the embarrassment go. It had been a long time since he'd popped in, since either of us had called to each other.

"I miss you," I said. "Are you still encamped?"

"I am. We are."

"Maybe I'll come visit you." An idea formed in my mind. I remembered my aborted attempt to contact Baird

151

with the ring, before Galfride had shown up. I had a strong urge to see all of them, and those places in the past where I'd neglected to return.

"Ye'd be welcome, my angel." Boldo sat by a fire, whittling.

"Okay, good. Then we could catch up." I paused. "Did you want something specific?"

"Just worryin' about ye," Boldo said. "Make sure to come see me."

"I will. I promise."

We let go of the connection. The times I'd been with him lately had been brief, fleeting, surrounded by enemies or fraught with disease and despair. It would be nice to just sit by a fire and talk.

I tapped gently on Marget's mind to see if she could talk.

"Yes, come over," she said, immediately.

I loved having a true friend in town, one who understood all I'd been experiencing.

This time, I popped over to her yard rather than walking, something that was becoming easier for me. Jumping from place to place in my own time, I had no fear of getting stuck in between.

"Come in," she called from her kitchen.

I came in and gave her a hug, then scooted into a chair at the table as she placed a warm cup of tea in front of me.

"God, it feels good to be here."

She lifted one serious brow in question. "What is it?"

"Oh." I gave a laugh that was just a breath. "Everyone else seemed to be hovering undetected in my head. I figured you were, too. I had an unexpected visitor."

"I suspected."

"What did you suspect?"

"When we hugged, I thought I felt a taint of Galfride's

energy on you."

"Good grief." My cheeks flushed.

"What happened?" she asked.

"It's strange." I tried to piece together his visit. "He seemed to want to talk to me about the feeling Esch gave him when we were on Ylva's mountain. But he also…"

As I struggled to put the conversation into words, she held her cup and waited, worry on her face.

"He said he wants to help protect Esch. But I don't feel like I can trust that."

"I don't either. Not yet anyway."

"He said he'd submit to Ylva examining his mind for truth or lies. I got a feeling…"

"Go on. A feeling?"

I sipped the calming herbal blend. "…that he was sincere. But you know he's such a conundrum."

"Yes, I do." She drank. "I feel like there's something else troubling you about his visit."

"It's not important." Now I did feel heat in my cheeks. "Okay, he kissed me."

Her face took on a funny mix of frown and question.

"Fine, we kissed. It wasn't coercive. In fact…" I stared down, tracing a pattern on the tablecloth. "I…may have participated."

"Well, he's a handsome man. But this is a funny turn of events after…"

"After what he did to Rousseau. I know." I sighed. "After everything he's done. I'm going to visit Baird. And Boldo. Also, Kyna."

Marget cocked her head, inviting more.

"I was thinking how I've kept plaiting my hair but never found out what that's about, never learned the messages, or took control of the knowledge I have riding around dormant in me." I traced a line with a drop of water. "Same with the clothes I weave. I see things in them. They give me something. Confidence, maybe. Something to do with magic. But I've never known if there was power in them. I've never taken control of traveling through time."

"Ye want tutelage."

"I do. I want to know more about my powers and to learn the hand signals, and—" I nodded. "I want to learn from you. Maybe stitchery from Gwynedd. Will you go with me? If we learned together…not that you don't know a lot already…but we could practice together and…that would be nice."

She reached across the table for my hand. "It would be nice. Let's do it."

I took in a grateful breath. "I thought we could start in Mora's camp."

Marget brightened. "I'd like that very much."

"Would you?" My heart sped up. "And I'd like to go to your Cornish home, maybe when you still lived there. Well, then you'd be there. Would that be weird?"

"It might be fun to watch myself." She sounded wistful.

"There's something else. Galfride asked if we have something in this time that we could take to help Esch. We have oxygen tanks, of course. But Ylva's put a dragon there to watch over. Maybe that's a better guard than anything we could set up, as humans. Maybe I shouldn't worry?"

Marget still held my hand. "You want to go see the place. Experience Esch's energy again."

"Well, yes. But I do worry that Thorgisl might still go after Esch. And about Shagfen, too. I'm a bit responsible since I was part of sending them back there."

"But she's so much healthier now," Marget said, surprised.

I sighed. "I can't stop worrying that Thorgisl might team up with Galfride, who might involve Ian, even pull my son in somehow, to bring Esch back. But I'm not sure at all, now, that Galfride is a threat. Even Thorgisl might not be." I said aloud the circular thinking that had been tying me in knots.

"Because he's absorbed with his dragon riding?"

"That might not last forever. He'll always crave new power, as far as we know, and what if he tries to build Frigon's power in his service?

"I want to get Ylva's take on it."

"I miss her mountain eyrie," Marget said.

What a strange vacation itinerary—a Traveler camp, a Cornish witch cottage, a Welsh tower, and Norwegian mountainside—all a thousand years ago.

"When do we go?" she asked, taking back her hand to clear our cups from the table.

"As soon as we want. Only twenty minutes or so will pass here. You could put a loaf of bread in the oven to be warm and ready to eat upon our return." I chuckled.

She clapped my shoulder. "I think we might make baked goods after we return, but funny to think about."

"I agree."

"Want to borrow a cape and just leave from here?" She bustled around, tidying, as if guests might pop in while we were gone. I guessed Ian could.

"Yes."

She hurried into the hallway where coats and capes hung on hooks. "Do you think we should tell everyone?"

"We can from Ylva's. Start there?"

"I like that.

A cold wind swept over us and I wished I'd taken the trouble to put on thermals at least. A wool jumper?

"Ylva can loan us something."

"Problem is, too much is collecting in my home. I need to deliberately plan a trip with a bundle of coats and sweaters."

I had sent Ylva a message that we were coming, if it was an okay time. She stepped out from the workshop at the base of their home with open arms, her long red coat sweeping in the gusts. "You chose a stormy time. Come inside."

We stomped up the steps to the main room. Duff sat at the table with a hot mug clutched in his great hands. He stood and embraced first me, then Marget.

"What brings ye to our mountaintop?" he asked.

"This and that. Concern about Esch. Galfride. The usual." I sat and the other three joined me.

"What's that no-good, foul meddler done now?"

Marget stepped in, as Ylva brought hard cheese and flat cracker-like discs to the table. "He actually seems to have offered his help in protecting Esch."

"Why would we need his help? Amgath is there to watch over Esch and Shagfen."

"True. I just felt like Thorgisl might still be a threat."

"That worm is no threat," Ylva said calmly, tucking cheese and cracker neatly into her mouth. She'd chewed and swallowed. "Was there something else on your mind?"

"Not yet. I want to—" I glanced at Marget. "—plan some training. For me. I plan to make the rounds. Check on Mora and her clan. Peek in on Kyna in the 12th century. Baird and Aelfwyn. And end up in Cornwall for Marget to show me more of her life there. I figure by the end of all that, I might come up with a good list of skills."

"What sorts of things do you have in mind?" Ylva asked, brows raised high on her forehead. She was all but rubbing her hands.

"Something tells me you might like some of this journey yourself," I said, grinning.

"You know I always luff a good new skill," she said, eager.

"Me, too," Marget said.

"Do I get to come this time?" Duff asked, shoving back from the table to stretch out his legs.

"For all of it?" I asked.

"Sure. I always wanted to see our home two centuries in the future. And I need to pop in on my brother and his lad. As for Mora and Boldo, and Talaith...they have a pipe tobacco I hanker to taste. Besides, I think Boldo owes me a tankard o' beer."

"Oh. Serious stuff." I winked at him.

"Serious, indeed. Do I get to see your home in Cornwall, Marget?"

"I think your head might knock down the loft," she said, nibbling a cracker. "These are yummy."

"I'll give you the recipe," Ylva said, standing. "When do we go?"

"I'll check what time of day it is." I slipped into the part of my mind connected to my boots, where Boldo resided. "Are you awake?" I asked, quietly.

"O' course I'm awake. T'is midday, angel." He brought down a hatchet on a wedge of wood, splitting it.

"Would you and your clan be open to a visit?"

"I'm amenable to seein' ye any time, Dawnlight."

"Thank you. Can I bring a few others? Marget, Duff and Ylva?"

"Yes, bring them all. I will tell Mora. We will have a

grand feast with music and dancing and the like."

"I don't want to put you to trouble."

"Dancing, trouble? Put me to trouble any time you like, Angel."

"Well, in that case."

"Come and brighten our camp, my angel."

"Where are they?" Duff asked as we broke our connection.

"I have no idea," I said.

Ylva's brows puckered.

"You'll just go to him?" Marget asked.

"That's how it's worked before. Like when I found him imprisoned in the Jutland cells. Shall we go?" I was excited to see the wagons, smell the smells. I'd mostly landed in the camp by accident, escaping from Galfride or trying to get elsewhere.

"I want to hunt around for gifts to bring," Ylva said, starting up the stairs.

"That's a nice idea," I said, feeling bad that I hadn't thought to bring anything myself.

Marget pulled her large woven bag in front of her and lifted out a bundle of baked goods.

"Oh wow. That was thoughtful of you." I sighed.

Chapter 19

It was for here or there, depending on where we spent most time. I also shoved in some herbs. If we'd gone to Cornwall first, I might have gathered more." She glanced at my expression. "You're gift enough for Boldo."

I laughed. "No. It's so gracious bringing things. Maybe I should go back and get something."

"Don't be silly. It takes a toll, you know, this travel through time."

"Does it?" I wondered.

"Would they likes some winter vegetables from the root cellar, do y' think?" Duff called upstairs to Ylva.

"Yes, bring some," came Ylva's voice from the floor above. Soon she came down with an armload of knitted items, a few carved objects, a small flute and more.

"Is it Christmas?" I asked.

"They'll love it," Marget said, pawing through the pile Ylva heaped on the table.

"Let's choose some. I have fun felt animals for the children."

We spent some time going through the choices until Duff came up from the cellar. "Ready?" He wore his travel cloak and took up a staff that leaned by the front door. He seemed happy. I thought he'd like a visit in the Wanderers' camp. After all, he'd spent much of his childhood that way.

"I am." I still wore my cape over my shoulders. They were far more acclimatized than I to the temperature even indoors. "Oh, I wonder if I might borrow a sweater?"

Ylva dug in a wood chest and held out knit hat, mittens, scarf, and sweater to me.

"You're too good," I said, accepting with glee. I pulled them all on.

Marget had all she needed packed into her bag.

I held out my hands. The others joined me and our minds slipped together. I shared my connection to Boldo with them as the sky turned dark. I felt only Marget and Ylva's hands, comforting in the oblivion between.

Then we stood in a clearing full of colorful caravan wagons, campfires, the busy bustle of Traveler life. Boldo strolled up, kerchief at his neck, and kissed both my cheeks. He and Duff embraced. He bowed to Ylva. I caught, in his mind, memories of her in the sea with us, removing the loathsome amber Thorgisl had embedded in his hand. He turned to Marget. "I've met you briefly," he said, pressing his hand to his chest and giving her a small bow of the head.

"Good to see you again," Marget beamed, cheeks dimpling.

More of the Silwy clan had come up behind Boldo, Mora at their front. I slipped through to her and hugged her for a long time. She had grown healthy, plumped out a bit, with a bloom in her cheeks. I felt such relief.

Mora had been there at times when I felt most alone, trying to travel through time, or escaping Galfride. Of all the women of the past, I felt perhaps most indebted and most warm with her.

She pressed her cheek to mine. "I would na' be here had it no' been for your determination," she said, quietly.

A child grasped her skirt and she laid a hand to the side of his head, rubbing his brown curls. She caressed his cheek. "My grandson. By his sister." She swatted Boldo's arm. "When're you gonna give me some?"

"Talaith?" I asked. "Is she here?" I wanted to ask her about the language of the hands, and hair-plaiting.

"Oh, aye, she be here. Somewhere. Lookin' fer herbs." Mora drew them toward the fire, making hand signals to the children and adults who'd come close, curious about the group who'd appeared, the man and woman of gargantuan height, and two more average-sized women.

We sat around fires, chattering away the afternoon. Travelers set mugs of cider and cakes on stumps within reach. Marget, next to me, shared remedies with healers but soon left to help with food preparation at other fires. Through sparse forest, the Silwy clan's homes could be seen.

Elders near me discussed recent events and expressed concerns for the future.

Boldo took Marget's place by me just as a man approached like déjà vu. I knew him, yet had never met him. I recognized the deep scar down his cheek from Rousseau's stories. His gaze settled on me, brows furrowing as I gaped at him, sure he was Otho, bandit of the ancient seas, who'd kidnapped Gwynedd and, much later, drawn my son to to him as his ship slid into a world without breathable air.

Boldo stood. "Cousin. Here are folk for ye t' meet."

Otho stepped toward me and reached out. Feeling queasy, I nonetheless returned his gesture and he kissed my hand.

"Ye look at me as if ye know me," he said, confusion on his face.

"I...saw pictures of you in others' heads," I said, which was the truth.

His brows went up and he seemed to appraise me anew.

I reviewed his crimes, stomach unsettled, but held back remarks regarding them. After all, he'd come back to his people and was trying to make amends. So I'd heard.

Mora broke in. "Son, these good folk aided in my rescue. This be Ylva. Marget be a Cornish...healer—over yonder helpin' with the supper fixin's. You know Duff."

Otho nodded to the others. He stepped past the fire to clap Duff on one arm and give him a half-hug. "May I join ye?"

Much as I'd been told about his recent transformation into goodness, I did not trust the man who'd done anything for hire and hurt many lives, had risked my son's safety under the spell of the stone that wanted only to return to its world. I glanced around at the creased faces of the clan leaders to see how they felt about him at their council discussion. It was hard to tell. Faces were not particularly open to me. Some looked wary.

I got up. "I'm going to see if any more help is needed, cutting or...fetching water." I started for where I'd seen Marget last.

"No need, Ceirwyn. Stay and talk," Mora called out to me.

I felt torn then and searched for a plausible excuse. "I just need to—" I pointed vaguely, figuring it could indicate a multitude of private possibilities, then turned away again, skirting another fire circle and stepping around children playing.

I found Marget a few fires over, sitting with a round

stump upturned flat side up, chopping onions. I settled next to her. "What can I do?"

"Tired of the village council proceedings?" she asked, handing me turnips and knife.

"Clever you, making off. How should I cut this?"

"Just small cubes."

"There was something else." My heart still hammered and my stomach jittered from the encounter with Otho. I'd held his image for so many years, despising the man who delivered a young Gwynedd to Galfride who held her in his spell. Then in past months my fury toward him had escalated with my own son's endangerment. I told her of Otho coming to the fire. "When I pictured coming here, I completely forgot Boldo'd said his cousin was here."

"That was months ago. You couldn't know."

"I could have asked. Even Ylva could have told me. It just slipped my mind."

"Do you feel danger from him now?" Marget pushed chopped onions into a wood bowl and took up potatoes. "They were so excited to get Ylva's root vegetables. They must always have to barter for them. They surely don't stay anywhere long enough to harvest."

I nodded. "They were. It was a good thought of Duff's. I don't exactly fear Otho. I just didn't want to talk, or even think, near him. I don't trust him yet, whatever they say about his changes."

A woman came and took the finished onion from Marget. She smiled at me.

"I'm known as Ceirwyn," I said, introducing myself.

"Kimbre," the woman said, ducking her head quickly and turning to add the onion to a pot bubbling at the next fire over.

We chopped and sliced and stirred until the sun sank

behind the distant hills.

"Will you wear some of our clothes for the dancing?" Mora asked, as I helped lay out settings on the long tables.

"Oh, sure." I followed Mora to her enclosed wagon where she outfitted me with skirts, jangly flashy strings, and a bright head scarf. She applied charcoal to line my eyes, then held up a mottled mirror that gave me a rippling, funhouse effect. I laughed but she crowed at the success of her job on me.

When we returned to the near-ready dinner scene, Marget was jealous so Kimbre led her off to another wagon in a grove of willows.

Marget returned, delighted with her reds and dark maroons, even kicky boots. We hugged, jingling.

As all approached the long tables, Ylva eyed us up and down.

"Get some for yourself!" I suggested, but she shook her head.

"I don't think they have my height. Anyway, I can dance perfectly well in what I'm wearing. She opened her full-length red cloak to reveal long embroidered skirt and paneled vest with appliques.

"I don't blame you. You have to show your beautiful clothing while dancing around the fire," I said.

A call went up for feasting to begin. The air was filled with mouth-watering smells from the long tables heaped with platters of roasted meats and veggies, spiced sauces, the homy scent of flat breads baked over fire, mead and ale in abundance. We climbed onto long benches. Lantern light flickered on familiar faces near me and across the table. I gulped a good swallow of amber ale feeling a tingle of contentment. This was all of my medieval experiences combined, right here in the forest. We had only partaken of the meal a short time, plates full and more passed around, when musicians began to play off to the side.

I stared as Baird walked toward us, old wizened healer Aelfwyn at his side.

"Ye weren't goin' t' start festivities like this without me, were ye?" He clapped Duff's huge shoulder—towering above most of the others, except Ylva, who matched his height—and winked at me.

It'd been months since I'd seen him, in that fraught time rescuing Mora, leader of the Silwy clan of Travelers who hosted us now. I sucked in a breath and set my tankard back on the table, worried I'd spill it with my shaking hand. He looked entirely beautiful to me, hair windswept and tangled, eyes gleaming and alive, cape as travel-worn as ever.

He came around to my side. "May I squeeze m'self in here?" he asked.

The row shifted for him. He stepped over the bench sat, wafting scents of road travel—wood fires, wild winds, the scents I associated with him. I wanted to be alone with Baird, far from others, as he gazed at me.

Mora handed him a full plate.

"My thanks, *modryb.*"

He called her aunt. That surprised me. I glanced from him to Boldo across the table but Boldo only smiled. Further down sat Otho. I wondered when Baird would notice him, and what his reaction would be. Hopefully there would be peace.

"Baird, you know Marget, right?"

Aelfwyn settled herself next to Marget, and they immediately began a lively discussion of which I only caught parts. I determined to hug Aelfwyn later.

"We've met a few times, aye." Baird nodded toward

Marget and she smiled.

"Good to see you," she said.

"You as well." He took a bit of a sort of pilaf dish and followed with a healthy downing of ale.

"And Ylva," I said. "Well, of course you know Ylva."

Baird eyed her with that blend of admiration and confusion that the Norwegian shamaness often engendered. He glanced between her and his brother, the two largest at the table by far. In fact, there'd been a brief discussion of whether larger spaces should be allowed for leg room, but in the end they just raised the table slightly with larger struts under.

My gaze drifted to the musicians as they struck up a livelier reel. I noticed for the first time that Hamelyn had come as well. He already played his fiddle, plates of food and jugs of ale situated near at hand.

There was so much to say between Baird and I, so much that would not be fitting for a dinner party. I scooped up a bite of turnip mash noticing Baird's hand near mine on the table. He moved his slightly so that our skin touched, and electricity shot through me. I sighed, glanced at his beloved face, saw his gaze rest on my hand, on the rings. The new amber one glowed in the candlelight, the one I was supposed to use to call him. Had I not tried? I was unsure if it had been deliberate, letting it rest dormant on me. The boots always connected me to Boldo naturally. But I also chose to call to him at times.

Why had this ring been such a conundrum? Almost an obligation. But now that he was here, I wanted nothing but to breathe him in, lay my head on his chest, talk about all that had occurred.

"I know," he said in a low voice just meant for me. "We've been distant and much has occurred. I knew ye'd call me if there be need."

"I would. Yes. I..." I glanced around the table. So much to be said. But not now.

Chapter 20

We ate and chatted amicably with those around us. I noticed Baird occasionally eyeing Otho. The sea captain occupied himself with a dark-eyed beauty next to him, giving her all his attention. That was just as well, I thought.

"I'm goin' to join the players. Will that be alright with you?" Baird asked me.

"Of course. You go."

I watched him stride across to the gathering of musicians. Dancing had begun. I stayed where I was to watch. Would we sleep there or go back to Ylva's home? I wondered. Looking around for our hosts, I saw the speckled pattern of a sylph fluttering in a tree nearby. The colors of this one were unusual, shades of pink, orange, and chartreuse. Its tune washed over me. But there was something special, and familiar in it. Definitely not Bedw. I took in a quick breath. A message was coming through to me. Sophie? The harder I stared, the less clear the figure became. And then the form and its message were gone.

Had I seen my daughter? Had she been able to travel to the middle ages for the first time? As a Sylph? Was she in danger? What had she tried to say? Maybe she was caught between. My stomach churned with questions.

Maybe I should return to my time now. But all the help was here, around me.

"Starin' int' the leaves, love?" Baird's voice came from behind me.

I turned to him.

"Care t' dance?" He held out a hand.

The sylph reappeared for just a moment. I thought I caught the message, "I'm okay, Mom. I know what I'm doing." She was gone again. I tried to relax and accept that she was not in danger. "I don't know if I have the energy," I said to Baird.

"I'll ask for a slow ballad." He pulled me in with the dancers as he motioned to the players, flicking a hand signal. The melody changed to something slow and sinuous. He ran his palm down my back and I shivered.

Kyna's knowledge must have kicked in as the music changed again. I seemed to know steps to a dance that many other dancers followed. I loved the feeling when I was at one with the culture, with Kyna's knowing. He twirled me out, my skirts furling. Strings of mirrors jangled.

I saw Talaith and again wondered where I might sleep. Maybe in her wagon. I hoped to finally learn from her about the sign language they used, and about plaiting messages into hair. Maybe tomorrow.

Baird ducked his head to my ear and whispered, "There's a wagon we might sleep in tonight, if ye did'na have other plans?" His breath tickled, stirring my insides.

I said chuckling, "No other plans," and slipped my arm around his waist.

"Good." His voice was throaty.

"But will we displace someone?" I asked.

"They were happy to shift," he said, his expression unreadable.

"Hmm…" I mused, quirking a brow. "Were they indeed?"

"Indeed, they were. Ylva and Duff're leavin' back t' their own home. Hamelyn's takin' Aelfwyn t' the tower. She wants t' sleep in her own bed."

"And Marget?"

"She wants t' stay. She's made fast friends with Kimbre who's trading beds around, combining a few little 'uns, I think."

"How do you find all this out?" I asked.

"Ah, people talk. Want t' slip away now?"

From a small window opening in the wagon we'd borrowed, I watched clouds scuttle across the low quarter moon. A few stars shone.

Baird turned on his side so that he snuggled to me, and stroked my hair off my ear. On one elbow, he said, "Has there been more keepin' ye distant?"

I turned to him, head on a pillow, face close to his. For a moment I didn't speak. The moon cast light across his chiseled face; his warm eyes studied mine, serious. "Maybe."

He sucked in a breath. "Ah. Maybe." His teeth showed but it was not a smile.

"I think…" I tried to find words I didn't even know myself. "I think I tend to withdraw when I see pain ahead."

"Ye see pain." It was a statement.

"Well, I…" I moved my fingers across his bare chest, smoothing the fine hairs, pressed my lips to the tender flesh in the hollow by his shoulder. "I can't stay long in your time. And I can't picture holding you in mine." I searched his face. "Maybe I'm selfish but I don't see a very relaxed future for either of us."

"Why can't ye picture holdin' me in yer time?" he asked, brow furrowed.

I smiled sadly. "You know how your time is different from mine. A lot of time can go by. I could come back to see you and…" The corners of my mouth tugged with emotion.

"I might be dead? Dove, we can use the rings t' stay connected. Is it…so important t' ye t' grow old predictably? Worth cuttin' me off from yer life?"

I gasped and shook my head. Put that way, the options were stark, real, and final. "Nope. Not worth it." I toughed his face, rested my hand along the cheek and jawbone, the beard I loved, cropped close, the strands of brown hair dusted with silver. I kissed him. We lingered.

He pulled away, studying me. "It's decided then?"

"What's decided?"

"You'll marry me."

My mouth went from laughter to bewildered, back to smile lines. Was he joking? "Marry. Baird, you're a thousand years ago. How can we marry?"

"Well, just fer our folk. A nice festive time like this one." He waved toward the dinner and dancing we'd recently partaken in. "Or…in your time, if ye prefer."

"Better for Sophie. But…I hadn't…"

"I want t' be with you, Dove." He cupped my face and kissed my lips he'd puckered with his hands, laughing. "Let's sleep." He slid his arms around my shoulders so my cheek pillowed on his sweet bicep.

I smelled his skin and kissed it. His lids drifted shut. I watched until they popped open again. "Ye gonna watch me all night, m' love?"

"Maybe not. I thought about it." I turned, nestled into him, and tried to enter dreamland. Giving up, I stared at the moon.

He stroked my hair one more time, then I heard his even breaths.

Marry him, I thought. "But you're never happy in my four walls, Baird," I mumbled thinking he slept.

"You want to learn more here in my time. I want t' learn more in yours."

"Like what? To play in a rock n roll band?"

"I can only imagine what that means. I want t' learn about that picture box." His voice was starting to drift off.

"Oh, my laptop." I grinned. "Okay. Yeah. There's a lot in there."

After that he was silent until there was the slightest bit of a snore. I pushed him on his side and pressed myself to his back. Eventually, I too slept.

Morning sounds greeted me through a fog of deep sleep. I was turned away, Baird's arms looped around me.

"Noisy buggers," he grumbled.

I reached for my skirt, felt around for other clothing items. "Gotta pee." I pulled reluctantly out of the warm embrace and covers, found my boots, and slid through the hide flaps.

Outside, I breathed in the sweet smells of forest and fires and headed between trees, away from the camp. Finding a sufficiently enclosed pocket, I squatted. "Hope this isn't a stinging nettle," I thought as I pulled off a soft leaf to wipe.

Marget came across the clearing toward me as I stepped from between trees.

"Don't you look a sight?" she said, ruffling my hair.

I put a hand to my head, half smiling. "Is there a place to clean up?"

"Yeah. Come on." She led me past fires. Baird sat at one, drinking from a horn cup.

I gave a quick wave—a flick of my hand—and hurried on. The land sloped down. I saw the creek for the first time.

Close to the water, an area was concealed behind blankets. A mother washed her baby in a tub by a fire. It was only women here. I stripped down to wash from warm water in a basin handed to me, with a chunk of brown soap. Marget did the same.

"How did you know about this?" I asked.

"Kimbre told me."

"The good thing about staying with women."

"Oh, I'm sure there had to be at least one good thing about staying the night with Baird," she said in a low voice with a conspiratorial wink.

"Snuggling was good," I said, pulling underclothes, skirt and blouse back on, then my boots. "I wonder where the clothes I came in are."

As we climbed the slight rise back to camp, I felt like I should mention Baird's proposal, or semi-, pseudo-proposal. But the weirdness of it that had plagued me from its inception stopped me: he was a thousand years ago. This world that surrounded us was a millennium in the past. I could marry in his time—that strange woman from the future who may or may not appear again. But what did it mean?

Did it matter? That was all the for-the-public aspect. He'd said he wanted to intertwine his life with mine.

That same day, Marget and I decided to return to modern time for our creature comforts.

"I'll come to ye soon," Baird said, intense. We'd said it many times before, and it had not happened. This time it carried a different weight.

I called Sophie. "Were you there? I thought you were. I thought I saw you and you spoke to me."

"I saw you Mom, in the gypsy clothes, dancing."

"I wanted you to be able to dance, too." My throat tightened.

"It's always beautiful to be a sylph, and to experience other times that way."

"Beautiful how?" I asked. I felt a little hurt that she acted so impersonal about seeing me there.

"Well, you know the feeling the sylph song gives. That's how it feels to be a sylph—all love, all healing and sweetness."

"But in that form, did you have the sense of knowing me?" I was trying to wrap my head around it. Why had she been chosen? There had to be something special about her. Of all of us, was she the closest to love and healing?

"I did. But differently from in my human form. More…detached."

I wanted to be happy for her but that scared me. What if she went so often that she forgot about us?

Next day, sitting out in Marget's yard, I asked what she knew about sylphs.

"I honestly don't know much about them. There might be more in Wales than in Cornwall."

"Even more in Scotland, according to Boldo and Baird."

I determined to get answers on my next trip to the past. But when I arrived home, Baird was there, sitting on my front porch.

"You can always let yourself in," I said, knowing he knew where the key was hidden in the back.

"That's alright. I ha'n't been 'ere long." He tossed a

long, tousled weed he'd been playing with onto the path. "Let's work out how we'll entwine our lives." He unfolded his long form.

"Oh. Okay." Panic sailed across my heart. Did I feel suffocated? Could I still come and go, play with Marget, visit others in the past? Talk to Boldo with my boots?

He took my hand, and my heart's rhythm shifted to a lower pounding. Bass drum.

"Come with me," I said. "I'll show you what Joaquin did with the attic."

I led him to the side staircase and we climbed. As we entered, I was acutely aware of who had last been there with me.

Baird admired the diamond shapes of cut glass set into the door before following me through the magical den and guest room to the balcony. Stepping to the rail, he stared out. "This be a fine addition. Ye can see the sea now." He kissed the top of my head. I felt his sense that the improvements would make a difference in his life as well. This was sharing. It was...good.

He turned and put his butt against the balustrade. "This be sturdy?" He glanced at the yard below.

"It better be." I shook it with both hands. "Feels sturdy."

"Aye, it does. I'm only playin' with ye, Dove. This be a guest room?"

"It does. It is."

We stepped inside and he looked around.

Chapter 21

T hank the gods Galfride and I hadn't ended up on that bed. It was extra-long in case Rousseau was sleeping there, as he had, several times. I thought it could even accommodate Ylva in length, though not with Duff as well. They could have my bed if they ever deigned to stay. The ceilings were now tall enough. Joaquin had been able to raise them to the roof level for a wide section down the middle of both upstairs rooms.

"And this is for scrying and rituals. It wouldn't fit the full Thirteen, I don't think, but I've got a small apothecary." I opened the armoire doors. Joaquin had fitted it out with tiny drawers. "Under here is my scrying bowl that Marget gave me." I lifted a curtain beneath a carved table. "I haven't quite decided how I want to set this up."

Baird whistled. "This be a fine room, love." He put a hand to my cheek and my heart rustled.

I'd been adding small shelves, some mounted to the walls, choosing objects from my travels, planning to add more over time. It felt good to show it to someone appreciative. Of course, my kids loved it, and Marget had seen it. She'd even offered ideas and brought me a few choice items from ancient Cornwall. I had artwork by Jarl, and Shelley had contributed a crushed glass mural that hung in a high window, casting colors over the room in a certain light.

"Seems well finished t' me. We could get a good circle in here." He seemed to be planning an invitation.

"What are you thinking of? Does The Thirteen need to meet? In another time dimension?"

He pushed back strands of my hair, stroked my temple with his fingertip. "I think there be a few concerns floatin' around in here, aye. As t' the time period in which they might be aired and contemplated, I'm not sure."

"What issues do you have in mind?"

There were two fluffy chairs in the corner. I took one and he sat in the other. Sensing a conversation coming that we might want to keep private, I built the protective sphere around us. Since I made the barrier often, it took little effort to make it solid.

"Esch's safety," he said, "And your daughter slippin' between times as sylph."

"You saw her? When we were with the Silwy?"

He nodded. "I was aware of her. I called to Bedw and asked if she was Sophie's guide. She said she could be. In her inimitable way, she conveyed that Soph has never gone between the times without her. If a new sylph be formed, the clan she joins is her clan for life. Or...swarm or some form o' groupin' like that."

"So Bedw will always know where Sophie is? And come to her if she's unsafe?"

"That's my sense of it." Baird crossed a long leg over his knee.

I huffed a small laugh. "I don't need The Thirteen here. I only need you." I drew in a breath, aware of recent incense, and the wood of the chest drawers.

"No' for that. But about Thorgisl. And Esch. And one more."

"One more?"

He'd brought up his fingers to count number three.

"Galfride."

I felt a blush creep in. "Galfride?" My voice squeaked and I cleared my throat. Traitor vocal cords!

His head tilted a fraction, as did his brow. "Galfride. And Ian. The kidnapping o' yer son?"

"Oh. That. Yes."

Baird sat forward, elbows to his knees, and contemplated my face, an inscrutable smirk playing across his features. "Somethin' t' tell me? Something else?"

"Oh. No. No, no."

Baird's hand rubbed across his mouth, maybe to wipe off a further grin. "That be…a lot o' protest, love."

I huffed a sigh. "Well, okay. Um. Galfride came over here, and seemed… You see, when we were all doing a sort of intervention, on Ylva's mountainside, Esch…" I hadn't ever explained this before to anyone in full. "Well, the stone felt angry. Galfride was furious, and I tapped into a sort of mountain-love that I'd discovered in the Alps. The time I was escaping from Galfride. You remember I built that crystal lance made of Ing runes—because of your daughter, Gwynedd's stitchery with the Ing, I guess it became a bit *my* rune."

The brand on my shoulder prickled as we spoke, as though it responded.

"Like your power rune. Or one of them."

"Yes." I nodded. "And it helped me shoot up through the mountain, or the mountain just parted for me but I kept going. Maybe that was the lance as well. Anyway, I felt huge love from the mountain. And that came back to me on *Galdhøpiggen*, Ylva's mountain. It seemed to combine with Esch. All of us felt a fantastic rush, in our hearts, all through us. Galfride changed, for a minute. Then he was surly again but I think the feeling never left him. So, he came over and asked me about that feeling. I thought he was going to hold me to giving him that feeling again, as if it was something I could create. I didn't want to tell him it was Esch and make him want the stone. I said it was a combination."

Baird followed all this with wary gaze, brows expressing a fluctuation of worries.

"He ended up saying he knows Esch is special and he'd want to protect it from Thorgisl too. He asked if there's a modern apparatus that would help humans breathe in that world."

Baird's eyebrows shot up.

"I know. Suspicion zinged, that he was playing me to get to the stone himself."

Baird nodded, like "duh".

I was approaching the weird moment, the kiss, and didn't want it to collide into the thoughts I was willing to share. Quickly I tucked the memory of the brief embrace behind my mind wall.

Did marriage mean I couldn't keep my wall? Surely not. He must have his own. I supposed we had to talk about it.

"Sounds like that's topic number four then."

"I think it falls under Numero Uno," I said, lifting an index finger. "Thorgisl and Esch. Which Ylva assures me is under control."

"Only one left? The Galfride-Ian debacle which has involved your son. Was your daughter threatened by him as well?"

"Maybe Ylva needs to give him a baby dragon," I quipped, feeling slightly guilty. I did not want to admit that there was a problem also in Galfride's focus on me. Was it on me, or the Stone? What was that kiss? But maybe I did have a solution. He needed a new focus. And not to be lonely.

Computers. Sophie could teach him to use one. But did I trust him to be on the internet? A man who loves to control minds, stir trouble, gain power over?

Forget it.

"Poor Dragon," Baird said, and opened his arms, inviting me to his lap. I snuggled in, and that was the end of that conversation.

Baird was there the next day when I received an email from an old colleague.

"Can we talk?" was all it said.

We skyped later that afternoon.

"The thing is," Colleen said. "We want you to head up a new program."

Some in the linguistics department had decided it was too stodgy.

"Integral studies, incorporating indigenous knowledge. Those aren't so way out anymore," my friend said. "You've been at the forefront of new ideas. We want to catch up, compete with forward-thinking colleges. Maybe have a cross-discipline with cultural anthropology."

"That sounds—"

Maybe she detected hesitation. She hurried on, "Including the ancient meanings of writing systems, runes that were more spiritual. Shamanic knowledge, all of that."

"Colleen, you don't have to convince me."

After we got off our call, I stared into the yard. Baird

came up behind me. I turned my face up to his. He must have seen something glowing because he engulfed me in a congratulatory hug.

"Feel like looking at houses in the Berkeley hills?" I asked.

He nodded. "Where the squirrels follow you?"

"That's the place," I said, a thousand ideas running through my mind. "I'll keep this place, come here a lot. Marget can come see me down there."

That evening found me sorting books, boxing some, putting others on the shelves in the den. They'd all come down from the attic for the new spaces. Baird had gone to the past for a commitment he'd made to sing. I didn't know how he'd keep track of the times. Hamelyn could always tell him. They were connected, as Boldo and I were, minds easily speaking across the millennium.

I stayed behind, wanting some time to think through this phenomenon of being a professor again. The new school year started in less than a month. A lot to process.

A knock came at the front door. I felt Galfride's mind-call.

Was he keeping track of when Baird was there?

I opened the door to him. We sat in the living room with tea.

"I think you went t' the past again," he said once we'd exchanged niceties. Not many.

"I did."

"Are you going to have a council, about Thorgisl, and the Stone?"

"What do you think is the level of threat?" I asked, curious.

"Frankly, I don't think he's overly focused on that now."

"His dragon?" I asked.

"Yeah, he's seldom at the castle." He pondered my face. "There's something different. What's happened?"

"I'm returning to my old university, to be professor again."

"You won't be here?"

"I'll be here some."

"That's good though?"

"It is good. I'm ready. And it'll be different now."

"Different how?"

I told him about the rigidness, the non-acceptance of my research on old language meanings, beyond the pragmatic, the concrete, the useful.

"You're going t' try t' convince them o' spellwork?"

I laughed. "One step at a time. I'm not sure this world is ready. But little by little, it might help a lot of the problems we face." I took my time examining his face. "Galfride, what about you and Ian? Will you be holding my son hostage again? Do I need to worry? Or can we come to some kind of agreement?"

Galfride crossed his leg over a knee. "Kay... Ceirwyn— Kay's not a proper name for anyone, not even a cat or a bird—"

I bowed my head to him. "I thank you for your bracing bluntness."

"Well, I'm no' goin' t' call ye Dove."

"Please don't." My head jerked up. "Have you been listening in?"

"Never."

His insistence was a little too vehement. I gave him a suspicious frown.

"Anyway, Ceirwyn, I like it here, in this time. Could I stay sometimes in your home? I'd keep it very nice, respect yer privacy and the like."

Was he serious? Galfride, in my home?

"We can figure something out. Are you satisfied with what you've found…as far as a new kind of friendship with Ian?"

"I need a new purpose."

"What was your old purpose?" I asked, only partially sardonic.

He leaned forward with a funny smile. "I did perform useful tasked at times, Ceirwyn."

"Like what?"

"Hey. I'm a scholar. And I have helpful magic. I've helped you at times."

"What do you picture as a good purpose now?" I asked.

"Well, I don't know. That's the problem."

The next day, Galfride came over and asked about the shed in my yard. Soon he had it outfitted for simple living. He could come and go along the side driveway.

Galfride, staying on my property? Was I mad?

But at some point, you have to say, *C'est la vie*. Or *hyn yw fy mywyd*, if you want to be Welsh about it.

Epilogue

Baird and I took a celebratory vacation to the past. We sang in a few castles. I invited Kyna to join us in our minds, to sing as well. She partook happily from the 12th century.

We visited the Silwy often. I finally learned the Welsh Traveler hand signs, and how to plait messages in my hair. I gathered my language notes from Kyna in the 1200s.

When we returned to the twenty-first century, Baird learned to Google.

I hadn't brought up Galfride's visit. Or the kiss. I was still baffled by it, and not at all ready to explain it.

I found myself happy to spend less time in the past. There was no need to stay the full five days, until I started to fade, I realized.

"Do you think there really is a problem with tearing the web too much, coming back and forth too often?"

"Dove, I wouldn't worry."

"Do you think I've changed the past irrevocably, by getting involved—saving Boldo and the like?"

"You are a part of history. Your trips *are* the past. They happened. How can we say one history is true and another not?"

"I think you're right."

We found a sweet cottage north of the university, on a tree-lined street with large healthy squirrels galore.

Sylphs found my garden and I took in their magic.

Rousseau and Sophie came over often. The family traveled to Pomo Bluffs whenever we could. Sometimes by car. Mostly not.

When Baird came to visit the university campus, his medieval style captivated one and all. He became a language expert. We explained that he was from a rural part of Wales that had not modernized; they may have opened their minds to most of my research, but...time travel? Maybe not yet.

Things were quite sublime until one day, Esch called out to me in panic, and would not stop.

THE END

Marie Judson is a Northern California native, with Masters degrees in depth psychology and education. She's been a fantasy reader since her teens and loves complex tales of symbols with buried meanings that hold wisdom for our modern time. She also adores tales that involve forbidden romance, which you will find in her books. She's been a coffee roaster, a high school teacher and a college professor. She loves singing harmony and tries to grow vegetables.

Follow her at **www.mariejudson.com**